TROUBLE-SHOOTER

Ramona Beach, Florida—a resort that just missed being popular. The people were too small-town. To them strangers meant trouble, and they had a sheriff who echoed the sentiment with a blackjack.

Once it had been my town. I was eighteen when they railroaded me out after some money was stolen. "Can't trust trash," they said. I'd never been back.

I'd traveled a lot since—Korea, South America, places a trouble-shooter for the State Department is sent. Then they told me my next assignment—Ramona Beach, Florida. I'd almost forgotten . . . "Can't trust trash."

I didn't want to go back—job or no job. It couldn't turn out right, not with people remembering, and me feeling the way I did. There was bound to be trouble.

Fawcett Books
by *John D. MacDonald:*

JOHN D. MacDONALD

DEADLY
WELCOME

FAWCETT GOLD MEDAL • NEW YORK

DEADLY WELCOME

Published by Fawcett Gold Medal Books, a unit of CBS Publications, the Consumer Publishing Division of CBS Inc.

ISBN: 0-449-13682-5

A shorter version of this work has appeared in COSMO-POLITAN magazine under the title "Ultimate Surprise."

Printed in the United States of America

19   18   17   16   15   14   13   12   11   10

chapter ONE

HE HAD BEEN on special assignment in Montevideo, had been there only a month when, without warning, they had cabled him home. He got Pan Am to Miami and Eastern to Washington. On the April morning after his arrival, he took his written report on his half-completed job to his chief of section at State, and made his verbal report to the chief and two of his aides, carefully concealing his surprise and irritation at being pulled off, and his curiosity at who might be assigned to complete the job. And his greater curiosity at what might be in store for him.

Shoemacher said to him, "Alex, I might say off the record that I do not approve of this sort of thing. I do not believe that any other agency should be entitled to reach down into my section and lift one of my better people. But, because I do not have the facts as to how important or necessary this action is, and because the orders came, quite bluntly, from upstairs, I am in no position to protest. The loan period is indefinite. When they return you, Alex, I will be curious to learn your opinion as to whether this was . . . necessary."

"Who wants me?"

"The name and room number is on this slip. A Colonel Presser. Pentagon. He'll see you at any time."

He taxied to the Pentagon and found Presser's office at eleven-thirty. The girl looked blank and aloof until he said he was Alexander Doyle and the colonel was expecting him. Then there was a quickness in her eyes.

5

After a short wait she told him he could go in. The Colonel was a pale, meaty man who arose and came around the corner of his bare desk to honor Alex with a heavy handshake.

"So glad to meet you, Mr. Doyle. And this is Captain Derres."

Alex shook the narrower hand of a small rumpled captain with a ferret face. They sat down, Alex across the desk from the colonel, the captain at the colonel's right. The only object on the bare desk was a black-cardboard file-folder. From where he sat Alex could clearly see the title tab of the folder. *Alexander M. Doyle.* And the never-to-be-forgotten army serial number.

"You are probably very curious as to what this is all about, Mr. Doyle. Let me say that whether our little venture is successful or not, I am most appreciative to State for their co-operation in this matter. And let me say also, Mr. Doyle, that there is no need for us to ask you any questions." He touched the folder with the tip of a thick white finger. "We have here all pertinent data. You will understand, before we are through, just why you are singularly suited for this mission."

"May I make a comment, Colonel? Before you begin?"

"Of course, Mr. Doyle."

"You used the word mission. And there is a sort of . . . cloak and dagger flavor about all this. I want you to understand that even though my work during the past three years has been . . . confidential and investigative, it hasn't been at all . . . dramatic. I mostly juggle a lot of papers. Add bits and pieces together. Sometimes I come up with answers. Usually I don't. What I'm trying to say is that I don't believe I have the . . . talent or training for anything very dramatic."

"There may well be . . . dramatic elements in this, to use your word, Mr. Doyle. But we feel you are perfect for our purposes. To begin then, does the name Colonel Crawford M'Gann mean anything to you?"

"Y-Yes, sir. Something to do with the missile program. A technical type."

"Age forty-five. West Point graduate. Flyer in World War II. Work at M.I.T. and Cal Tech after the war. A brave and resourceful and . . . rather humorless officer. Cold. Brilliant. Could get to the heart of a technical problem and improvise measures to cure the bugs. A perfect man for these times. A driver. We'll give you a file on all this for your study, Mr. Doyle. I'll tell you the history briefly. Crawford was rather naïve about women. Three years ago he met and fell in love with a woman who was singing some . . . rather questionable songs in a supper club here. In spite of all the subtle pressure his friends could exert, he married her. We thought her a most unsuitable person. But, to our surprise and pleasure, she did a good job of making herself over into an army . . . rather an Air Force wife. Entertained properly. Handled herself well. And Crawford M'Gann's work improved, if anything. A year and a half ago, in November, M'Gann suffered a massive coronary. He did not die. He was given a medical discharge. His wife nursed him. She took him away to a secluded spot. She played the part of the diligent loving wife for a few months, and then it would appear that she became restless. It became necessary for Colonel M'Gann's sister to come and help care for him. November of last year, Mrs. M'Gann was murdered. The case has not been solved. I personally doubt that it ever will be. It is our desire that Colonel M'Gann return to Washington. He is not well enough to be placed on limited service, but he is well enough to operate in a civilian capacity and give us the benefit of his enormous talents. We need the man, Mr. Doyle. The country needs the man, badly. He is too involved with the murder of his wife to consider anything else. We need someone to change his mind. We think you are the man."

Doyle stared at the colonel and wondered if the man was mad. "But this is absurd, sir!"

"Perhaps I've been playing a rather stupid game with you, Mr. Doyle. I've left out certain essential facts. Colonel M'Gann lives with his sister in a rented beach cottage at Ramona Beach, Florida. The maiden name of the woman he married was Larkin. Jenna Larkin."

Alexander Doyle looked down at his hands and saw that he had clenched them into fists, that the knuckles were white with pressure. He felt as if he had been clubbed across the belly. The colonel and the captain seemed far away, and he knew they were watching him. He slowly became aware of the fact that the colonel was speaking.

". . . send other people down there, but it has been an utter failure. They have been strangers. The local officers of the law have chased them out. Celia M'Gann, the sister, has kept them from seeing the colonel. She thinks we . . . want to bring him up here and kill him. I'll be frank. Sustained work might cause his death. But if he were not still under the influence of his dead wife, I know it is a risk he would accept. That town of Ramona seems to . . . unite against anyone from outside. Our research on you shows you were out of the country when the murder occurred, Mr. Doyle. Otherwise you would have known of it. It received a big and unfortunately gaudy play in the papers. And it has made good copy for those magazines who trade on the sensational. There is a complete file of clippings in the folder we will give you."

"I can't go back there," he said simply.

Colonel Presser ignored his statement. "Because you were born and grew up in Ramona, Mr. Doyle, you will be able to fit into the community with little trouble. And it should not be difficult to devise a reasonable cover story to account for your presence."

"But I . . ."

"If the murder of Jenna M'Gann were to be solved, I suspect that Crawford M'Gann would come out of his morbid trance, but that is a little too much to hope for. It is hoped that you can . . . penetrate the defenses set up by Celia M'Gann and make an opportunity to talk in private to Colonel M'Gann. You will find in your folder the suggested line you should take in talking to him. She intercepts his mail. There is no phone at the cottage. We think that if an intelligent and persuasive man can get to him and talk privately to him, he may listen. And if he will not listen to the . . . call of duty, if I may be so trite as to call it that, he may listen to enough of the unpleasant facts about Jenna M'Gann to . . . weaken his preoccupation. The results of our detailed investigation of her are also in your folder, Mr. Doyle."

"But I don't think you understand."

"What don't we understand, Mr. Doyle?"

"I . . . I was born there, Colonel. Right at the bottom. Swamp cracker, Colonel. My God, even talking about it, I can hear the accent coming back. Rickets and undernourishment and patched jeans. Side meat and black-eyed peas. A cracker shack on Chaney's Bayou two miles from town. There was me and my brother. Rafe was older. He and my pa drowned when I was ten. Out netting mackerel by moonlight and nobody knew what happened except they'd both drink when they were out netting. Then Ma and I moved into town, and we had a shed room out in back of the Ramona Hotel and she worked there. She died when I was thirteen, Colonel. In her sleep and I found her. She was just over forty and she was an old, old woman. The Ducklins were distant kin and they took me in and I worked in their store for them all the time I wasn't in school. I don't even think of Ramona any more. Sometimes I find myself remembering, and I make myself stop."

"Are you trying to tell us you are ashamed of your

origin, Doyle? And that's why you don't want to go back?"

"No, sir. I'm not ashamed. We did as well as we could. It was . . . something else. The way I left. What they'll think of me down there. I was eighteen, sir. Just turned eighteen. That was 1944 and I was about to enlist. I was going on over to Davis, that's the county seat of Ramona County, and enlist on a Monday. There was a party on Saturday night. Sort of a going away party, sir. And I got drunk for the first time in my life. I passed out. I've thought a lot about the way it must have happened. I had a key to Ducklin's. I think somebody took it out of my pants and went and opened the place up and took the money and a lot of other stuff. Then put the key back in my pants and a little bit of the money. So . . . I ended up over in the county jail in Davis. I kept saying I didn't do it. I knew I didn't do it. I knew what they were all saying. That the Ducklins had taken me in and been decent to me, and that was the way I'd paid them back. Like all the rest of the Doyles. Can't trust that trash. And I'd never stolen anything in my life. And it was the first time I'd ever been drunk. And the last time I've ever been that drunk. I was a confused kid, Colonel. They talked to me over there. They said that if I'd promise to enlist, the judge would suspend the sentence. And I should plead guilty. So I did and he suspended sentence and I enlisted and they took me right away and I never went back, even to get my things. Not that there was much to get. I . . . I want you to understand, Colonel. I can't go back. Maybe it's . . . too important in my mind, more important than it should be. But I was . . . proud of myself, I guess. I'd made a good record in Ramona High School. Scholarship and athletics. I was popular with . . . the better class of kids. And then . . . it all went wrong for me. What will they say to me if I go back?"

The colonel stared heavily at him, then slapped the

black file-folder with a hard white hand. "I cannot make speeches. I can tell you some facts. You are thirty-three, unmarried. You have no close relatives in Ramona. The incident you speak of took place fifteen years ago. I can appreciate the depth of the . . . psychic scar. You enlisted too late to see action in World War II. From 1946 to 1950 you attended college on the G.I. Bill, after getting the equivalent of your high-school diploma while you were in the service. After college you were in the Korean action. During the two months before you were wounded in the left bicep by a mortar fragment, you were a competent patrol leader. You were given a bronze star. After your discharge, you passed competitive examinations and went to work for State on a civil service basis. You have received regular promotions. Three years ago you were placed on the kind of investigative work you are now doing. They think highly of you over there. We had the Veterans' Administration run a hell of a lot of cards through their I.B.M. sorters to come up with seventy-one possibles from Ramona and the immediate area on the west coast of Florida. We eliminated seventy. We were extraordinarily pleased to find you, Mr. Doyle, as we did not expect to find anyone so curiously well qualified for what we have in mind. We had to go very high to get permission to borrow you from State. This is not a make-work project, Mr. Doyle. I shall wave the flag in your face, sir. There are no indispensable men. But Colonel M'Gann comes as close to that category as anyone I should care to name. Meager as is your chance of success, it is an action we must take. Were this a police state, the problem would not exist. We would merely go down and get him in the middle of the night and bring him back. Under this form of government, he must come willingly. Other methods of persuasion have failed. This was Captain Derres's idea, to use a local person. I find it a good idea. And now Mr. Doyle, you propose that because of an adolescent traumatic experience, we should salve your tender feelings by giving up the whole idea?"

"Colonel, I . . ."

"You have security clearance. You have demonstrated that you have qualities of intelligence and imagination. As a matter of fact, I should think you would get a certain amount of satisfaction in showing the people of Ramona what has happened to that Doyle boy. Have you ever been in touch with anyone down there since you left?"

"No, sir."

"Have you ever run into anyone from Ramona?"

"No, sir. I've always been afraid I would."

The colonel opened a lower drawer of his desk and took out a fabricoid zipper folder, thick with papers. He thumped it onto the desk. "This is the material which has been prepared for you under the direction of Captain Derres, Mr. Doyle. I suggest you go through it carefully and come in here tomorrow at two o'clock. You can give us your answer at that time. If it is yes, and I hope it will be, you might give some thought to a cover story before you come in. As one factor you should consider in composing a cover story, please be informed that you will be supplied with ample funds out of an appropriation where strict accounting is not required by the G.A.O."

"Mr. Doyle," Captain Derres said in a soft and humble voice, "I should not want you to construe this as any sort of threat, you understand. I merely make a comment for your guidance. After the extraordinary measures taken to borrow your services, it would seem most odd to your superiors if you were to return immediately for reassignment. They would wonder in what way we found you unsuitable. And it would be only human for them to wonder again when considering future assignments and promotions. On the other hand, your

efforts for us, regardless of success, will result in a
. . . pleasant addition to your file." He smiled thinly.
"I am assuming you have your normal share of ambition.
Colonel, did you mention his contacting us?"

"I didn't. Thank you for reminding me, Jerry. Mr.
Doyle, I am afraid that you will be completely on your
own. There are good reasons for that which I cannot go
into. As far as official records are concerned, you will
be on leave of absence from State. If you get into any
sort of trouble, it will be up to you to get out of it.
We will be unable to replenish your funds should you
run out, but we will be able to reimburse you later for
any monies you use out of your own savings. At some
point you will either achieve success or become convinced that you cannot accomplish anything. You will
then, without delay, telephone this office and talk to
either Captain Derres or myself. Whoever answers will
make an inquiry as to your health. If you are successful, say that you are feeling good. If not, complain of
illness. After we receive the call we will inform State
that you will be reporting back to them shortly for reassignment. In the event of failure, we will wish to question you after you have returned. If you succeed, it is
unlikely you will see either of us again."

He took the heavy folder back to his hotel. By eight
o'clock that evening he had absorbed all of it. He knew
how Jenna had died. He knew what they wanted him
to say to Crawford M'Gann. With the instinctive caution of long training, he left the folder in the hotel
safe and went out into the April evening to walk the sultry
streets during the first heat wave of the season.

He had come back a long way, from autumn in Uru-
guay to spring in Washington. And further than that.
Back to the pine and palmetto scrub lands, and the night
sounds of that land. The whippoorwill and the mourn-
ing dove singing counterpoint to the dirge of the tree
toads. Water lapping the pilings of the decaying dock

and slapping the old hull of the net boat. The grinding whine of skeeters close to your ear. And, often, the muted grunting bray of a gator back in the slough.

He walked steadily, unaware of direction. There had been all the years of painful accretion of the new identity. He had thought it all so sound. He had believed it to be the real Alex Doyle. But now it was all beginning to flake away. Bits falling from a plaster statue to reveal once again that scared, confused and indignant kid.

He wondered what it had been like for Jenna to go back. What special torment it had been for her. Because she had been the first to leave. Six months before he left. They had been but one day apart in age, and he had been the elder. Left with a sailor, a Tampa boy on leave who kept driving all the way down to Ramona in a junk car to see her, and had finally driven away with her and never come back. A town scandal. That Larkin girl. The wild one. And old Spence Larkin had been nearly out of his mind because she had been the eldest child and his favorite. A mean and stingy old bastard. Treated the younger two like dirt and was always buying something for Jenna.

The wild one. Talk of the county. They couldn't control her. A little blonde with so much life in her, body turning to perfection at thirteen. All that recklessness and that high yell of silver laughter in the night. Up and down the county, carloads of them, at a hundred miles an hour, heaving the beer cans and the bottles into the ditch. Go way up to a dance in Venice and, the very same night, roar on down to the south, to a dance in Fort Myers.

He remembered how he'd known her without knowing her. Daughter of Spence Larkin. Old bastard has more bucks squirreled away than you'll see in your whole life, Doyle. She'd come in with a gang and sit at the counter at Ducklin's and she'd say, "Hello there, Alex." But they didn't know each other. And he would hear them talking dirty about her, at Ducklin's and at the school. "You don't have no chore getting the pants off Jenna, Herbie. She don't wear none, boy." It would give him a feeling of sickness and anger, and he didn't want to hear it and yet he did.

Then, in the Arcadia game in his sophomore year, when Bowers was hurt and they sent him in, he became a personage. He'd had his full height then, one inch over six feet, but he had weighed only a hundred and fifty-five. But it was all hard, fibrous muscle, and there had been a lot to prove, and this was the time. The chance.

And he had become part of the group, running with them when he had time off from the store, accepted. In the group with Jenna, and closer to her. Didn't think she would say yes to a date. Didn't ask for one. She asked him. Spence had given her a fast little run-about. He had taken it in on a trade at the boat yard and had it put back in shape. She asked him, in the store, on a Saturday night when they all stopped in. Asked when the others were talking and couldn't hear. "Come to the yard tomorrow morning, Alex. About ten. We'll try out the *Banshee*. Make a picnic out of it."

They took it down the bay, down between the mainland and the south end of Ramona Key, and then out through the tidal chop and Windy Pass, and then, running outside in the Gulf, down most of the deserted length of Kelly Key and anchoring it just off a wide white beach, anchoring it in the shallows and wading ashore with the beer and food and blankets and her little red portable radio. A strange day, unbelievable that he was alone with her. They took turns changing to swim suits behind a screen of sea grapes. Casual talk and some laughter. Swimming and sandwiches and beer. A strange day of mounting tensions, in glance and accidental touch. With the strain mounting between them until, at dusk, she was in his arms whispering that she thought he would never never try. He had been scared as well as wanting. He hoped they had been wrong—all that talk. He hoped they had been making it all up about her.

But she rolled away and took off the damp green and white swim suit and she was there for a little time to be looked at, and he somehow did not want to look at her but could not look away, until she rolled back to him with a little raw laugh and hungry mouth. He was virgin yet felt he should be gentle and tender because she was such a small girl. But tenderness was not her need. And even as he held her in that ultimate closeness, he had known with a wisdom beyond his years that he still did not know Jenna Larkin, that perhaps no one could know her. And in this union she had contrived, he was but an instrument of her restlessness and protest.

He drove the little *Banshee* home through dark familiar waters, her head on his shoulder while they sang old songs, sleepy with the sun, the swimming, the beer and the love. Very sophisticated. Making no direct reference to what had happened between them. Her car was at the yard, and when she dropped him off at the Ducklin house and responded so completely to his kiss, he asked her when he could have another date, sensing that "date" was now a new word for him.

"I don't know, Alex. Sometime, I guess. You ask me, hear?"

"I'll ask you."

When he was in bed with the lights off that night, it all seemed unreal, and he tried to encompass the enormous realization that It had finally happened to him, and It had happened with Jenna Larkin. He lay in the dark with his eyes wide, and went over each vivid fragment of memory right up to the point where he had not been aware of anything in the world, and beyond that to where he had been aware of her again, watching him with a strange intensity. He tried to think how the next date would be, and he tried to feel anticipation. But he merely felt sleepy and uncomprehending, and subtly soiled.

He tried to date her again, but he had little time off, and when he did, she was busy. And about two months after the picnic trip in the *Banshee* she was gone. With the sailor. The talk about her was worse after she was gone. Once he came close to joining in, letting them know that he hadn't been left out. But at the last moment he had turned away, bitterly ashamed of himself.

Since that time he had often wondered if Spence had found her and brought her back to Ramona. The dossier on Jenna, part of the thick file Colonel Presser had given him, answered the question. She had not come back. It covered the years from when she was eighteen until she was thirty, when M'Gann had met her. Had he read it about some strange woman he would have thought it unsavory in the extreme. A marriage and divorce. Modeling for life classes and seedy photographers and unsuccessful commercial artists. Singing with third-rate groups and in grubby joints. A police record of sorts. The minor night-time offenses for which you can be picked up in Seattle and Biloxi, Buffalo and Scranton. But it was all because she had been so alive . . . and restless.

So how had she felt when she had gone back? As the colonel's lady. Full of an uneasy bravado? Amused, perhaps? Why had she gone back there at all? There had been no need.

chapter TWO

AFTER LUNCH the next day he got the folder from the hotel manager and went to the Pentagon. He told them he had decided to do it. He did not tell them why. He did not tell them that he had learned in the long and sleepless hours of the night that if he did not go back he would spend the rest of his life in a half-world where neither identity fitted him, neither the old nor the new. He could not say that this was, in a sense, his own search for Alexander Doyle.

When he said he would rather not take the file with him, they both questioned him sharply until they were satisfied that he had retained all the information he needed to know. "And what about a cover story, Mr. Doyle?"

"I've got one that I think is very ordinary and very foolproof, sir. I know South America pretty well. And I know heavy construction equipment. On my last assignment I was working outdoors. And I look it, I guess. A lot of single men take construction jobs abroad for the high pay, and then go back to their home towns. If I had the passport and necessary papers to show I'd been in Venezuela for the last three years . . ."

"Sounds good enough. Get rolling on that, Jerry. Mr. Doyle, what will be your public reason for going back to Ramona?"

"Tired of knocking around. Got a few bucks saved up. Looking around with the idea of maybe setting myself up in a small business. If it hasn't changed too much, I'll rent a cottage out on Ramona Beach. That will put me closer to Colonel M'Gann. After I get established, I'll have to play it by ear. Maybe I can line up some kind of temporary job that will make it easier to get to the colonel. I'll need mobility, Colonel Presser. I think the best thing would be to fly to Tampa and pick up the right kind of clothes there and a used car. I don't think I was expected to amount to very much. Except for having some cash, I don't think I want to disappoint them."

"You sound bitter, Mr. Doyle."

"A little. Maybe. But I'll be a lot less conspicuous than if I went into town driving a rental sedan and wearing a suit like this one, sir."

"You are absolutely right, Mr. Doyle. I approve the plan. It isn't theatrical. You won't be tripped by the casual question. And you can look and play the part, I'm sure. When can we have his papers ready, Jerry?"

"By tomorrow noon, Colonel."

"We want you to take all the time you need to handle it carefully, Mr. Doyle. I think three thousand dollars would be ample."

"More than enough."

"How would you take it with you? Traveler's checks?"

"Alex Doyle, construction bum, would wear a money belt, sir. Or he wouldn't have any cash to bring back with him."

Presser laughed his approval. "Come in a little before noon tomorrow."

He bought the three-hundred-dollar Dodge off a Tampa lot late on Monday afternoon, the thirteenth day of April. He didn't want to arrive in Ramona after dark, so that evening he drove down as far as Sarasota and found a second-class motel south of the city on the Tamiami Trail. Ever since he left Washington he had been trying to fit himself into the part he would play.

That night, when he was ready for bed, he carefully inspected the stranger in the bathroom mirror. The sandy hair had been cropped short and the gray at the temples was now practically invisible. The eyes were a pale gray-blue. It was a long face, subtly stamped with the melancholy of lonely tasks. A big nose and a stubborn shelving of jaw. A sallow facial texture that took a deep tan and kept it. Twisty scar at the left corner of the broad mouth. A flat, hard, rangy body, with big feet and knobbed wrists and big freckled hands.

He studied the stranger and said quite softly, "Banged

around here and there. Have driven shovels and Euclids
and cats. And some deep-well work."

The face looked back at him, passive, somewhat secretive, with a hidden pride and hint of wildness.

He stretched out in the dark and listened to the
trucks go by just beyond his window. There was a
band of moonlight in the room. And air scented with
diesel fuel and jasmine. This was home land. And
different. Sarasota had turned from sleepy village to
busy tourist center. Ramona would be changed too. But
not as much. It was miles off the Tamiami Trail.

Tomorrow he would drive into town, right down Bay
Street. His hands were sweaty. He could hear the knocking of his heart. And he was a kid in a cell in Davis,
wondering what they were going to do to him.

At ten o'clock on Tuesday morning he turned off
Route 41 onto State Road 978, moving slowly through
the bright hot morning, through soaring throngs of
mosquito hawks, through flat scrub land with occasional
oak hammocks and some tall stands of slash pine. The
last time he had come over this road he had been going
the other way, fast, in a back seat between two deputies,
dog-sick and trying not to sniffle. They had stopped to let
him be sick at the side of the road while the deputies
talked in soft slow voices about the hunting season. He
remembered wondering if they were wishing he'd try to
run.

About four miles from town he came upon the first
change. A huge tract had been cleared and shell roads
had been put in, but now the scrub was growing up
again. A big faded sign said that it was *Ramona Heights.
Florida Living at a Reasonable Price. Big Quarter-Acre
Lots at $300. Ten Dollars Down. Title Insurance. See
Your Broker*. The roads were named after the states of
the union, and the road signs were so faded as to be almost illegible. He could see a few scattered houses,

small cinder-block structures painted in brave bright colors.

Farther on he came on new houses where it had all been pasture land, and then some drive-ins and motels and a small shopping section. More houses, and a new school of blond stone and glass, with the yellow buses ranked outside it. And then, ahead of him, he could see where the trees started, the big live oaks, bearded with Spanish moss, that shaded the east end of Bay Street. They were the memorial oaks, planted right after the first World War, and to him they had always marked the edge of town.

He drove along the shade of Bay Street, past the old frame houses and the old stucco houses of the boom of long ago, and he read the forgotten names of the side streets. And then he was back in sunlight again, where the street widened, looking along the three blocks of the business center toward the blue water of Ramona Bay, bisected by the causeway and old wooden bridge that, as a continuation of Bay Street, provided access to Ramona Key and Ramona Beach.

The old hotel was still there with its broad porches, but the stores across from it had been torn down and replaced by a chain supermarket set well back, a big parking lot, orange parking lines vivid against asphalt, in front of it. Cars dozed in the sun. A pregnant woman walked tiredly toward a dusty station wagon, followed by a boy in a soiled white apron pushing a supermarket cart containing two big bags of groceries. A grubby little girl sat on the curbing in front of the telephone office, solemnly licking a big pink icecream cone. Cars were parked diagonally in the sun on either side of Bay Street, noses patient against the curbing. There was a new bright plastic front on Bolley's Hardware. Where Stimson's Appliance had been there was a big shiny gas station where two fat red-faced men stood drinking Cokes and watching an attendant check the oil on a Chrysler with Ohio plates.

He read the lawyer names and the doctor names on the second-floor windows of the Gordon Building, and a lot of them were different, but a lot of them could be remembered.

The Castle Theater was closed, boarded up. There was a new dime store. And now they had parking meters.

He looked at Ducklin's Sundries. It was bigger. It had taken over the feed store, and the whole front was an expanse of cream and crimson plastic and big windows. He parked in front of it. Getting out of the car and walking in was one of the most difficult things he had ever done. It was frigidly air-conditioned. An old man who looked vaguely familiar stood by a big magazine rack mumbling to himself as he read a comic book. Two young women sat at the counter with their packages, eating sundaes. There was a pimpled young girl in a yellow nylon uniform behind the counter, scraping the grill with a spatula, slowly and listlessly. A young man sat on his heels by a center counter, taking items out of a carton and stacking them on a shelf. Alex Doyle knew no one.

He walked to the counter and slid onto one of the red stools. The pimpled girl glanced at him and dropped the spatula, wiped her hands on her apron and came over.

"Coffee," he said. "Black." When she brought the coffee he said, "Is Joe or Myra around?"

"Joe? Myra? I don't get it."

"Mr. or Mrs. Ducklin," he said.

"They don't own it any more," the girl said. "You want to see the owner, it's Mr. Ellman and he isn't in."

The young housewives had apparently overheard the conversation. "Pardon me, but Joe Ducklin died a long time ago. Oh, ten years anyway. She ran it for a while and then she sold out, a couple years later I guess it was. It's kinda creepy, somebody asking for Joe. Pardon me. I mean it just sounded creepy. You know."

"I used to live here."

She was a heavy young matron, hippy, with a rather coarse face and a dab of chocolate on her chin. "I've been right here my whole life long, so if you lived here I guess maybe I ought to know you." She laughed in a rather disturbingly coy way.

"I used to work in this store," he said.

The other woman peered at him intently. "You wouldn't . . . you couldn't possibly be Alex Doyle? You must be!" She was a sallow blonde with a long upper lip.

"You're right."

"Well, I wouldn't guess you'd know me because I was just a little bit of a thing, but I sure remember you coming over to the house to see Jody. Jody Burch. I'm one of Jody's kid sisters. I'm Junie. Now I'm Junie Hillyard. I don't know if you remember Billy Hillyard. And this here is my best girl friend, Kathy Hubbard, who used to be Kathy King."

"I . . . I don't remember Billy Hillyard, except as a name. But I certainly remember Jody. Does he live here?"

"Jody's dead," she said. "He liked the navy so good he stayed in, and it was just three years ago and he was on a supply ship and they were loading something and something broke and they dropped it on him. It was a terrible thing. He had thirteen years in and he was only going to stay twenty."

"I'm sorry to hear it."

"It just about broke us all up. His wife is married again. She sure didn't wait long, that one. She wasn't local so you wouldn't know her. A Philadelphia girl."

"Does Myra Ducklin still live in town?"

"Why, she surely does! She's right over on Palm Street in that house they always had. I just remembered you're kin to her, somehow, and you used to live there so I guess I don't have to tell you . . ."

She stopped abruptly and her eyes grew round, and

Doyle knew that she had suddenly remembered all the rest of it. She leaned close to her friend and whispered to her, rudely and at length. Then Mrs. Kathy Hubbard turned and stared at him also.

They had finished their sundaes and their money was on the counter. They stood up and Junie cleared her throat and said, "Are you really sure Mrs. Ducklin would want to see you?"

"I wouldn't know."

"Are you on a vacation?"

"I might move back here, Junie. Care to advise me?"

"Maybe you'd feel more at home if you settled down at Bucket Bay, Alex Doyle." They walked out with great dignity. And stared at him through the windows as they walked toward their car with the packages. Junie had the intense look of the confirmed gossip. The self-righteous gossip. That Alex Doyle has come back here, bold as brass, and what are decent people going to do about it? He had the nerve to speak to me. Robbed his kin and they let him run away into the army and here he is right back again after all this time. Cheap sporty shirt and snappy slacks. Tough looking.

He put a dime beside the empty cup and as he got up and turned to go, a big old man, sweaty and slow-moving, came in out of the sidewalk heat, patting his broad forehead with a blue bandanna. Jeff Ellandon. Perennial mayor of Ramona. Fifteen years heavier and slower.

He looked at Doyle with shrewd old eyes, stuffed the bandanna in his pocket and said, in a voice frayed and thin with age, "Guess I should know you, son. Guess my memory is about to give out on me. You one of the Bookers?"

"Doyle, Judge. Alex Doyle."

"Well sure now. Bert's boy. There was you and Rafe, and he was the older one, got drownded with Bert that time. Mother was Mary Ann Elder from up in Osprey. Come and set, son."

Alex followed the man back to a small booth and sat facing him. He ordered another cup of coffee and Judge Ellandon had a double order of chocolate ice cream.

"Been away for some time, I'd say, son. You were the one had that trouble. You worked right here, come to think of it. Joe Ducklin was a second cousin of your daddy. I remember Joe cussin' you almost right up to the time he died. Stingy old rascal. He and Spence Larkin were the closest men in town. The way I figured it, you were just collecting back wages, son. I guess you can see the town ain't changed much."

"I saw a lot of new stuff when I drove in, Judge."

"I guess we must have had maybe fifteen hundred people when you left and we haven't got more than seventeen, eighteen hundred right now. Everybody else growing up big north and south of us and we keep poking along. No future here, son. It's those dang Jansons."

It was a story Alex had long been familiar with, the favorite gripe of local businessmen and boosters. At the turn of the century a wealthy sportsman named Janson had come down from Chicago to fish. He bought land on the north end of Ramona Key and built a fishing lodge. When Alex had been little the kids believed the old corroding structure was haunted. It had burned down when he had been about nine years old. Janson had been the one who financed the causeway and bridge to Ramona Key. And he had so believed in the future of the area that, for a sickeningly small sum, he had purchased all of Ramona Key except for a three-quarter-mile strip of Gulf to bay land just opposite the causeway, all seven miles of Kelly Key, and huge mainland tracts on either side of the sleepy fishing village. Janson had died during the first World War, and the estate had been tied up in litigation for many years. At the time of the Florida boom there were plans to subdivide and sell off the Janson lands, but the boom collapsed before any action was taken. Since then any attempt to buy any Janson land had been met with stony indifferent silence.

"They still won't sell any off, Judge?"

He snorted with ancient fury. "Got all the money in the world. Don't want more. Don't give a damn the town is strangled. Can't grow except to the east into the piny woods. Nobody's going to come in here with big money and put up the kind of stuff that'll bring the tourists and make the town grow, not with that little bitty piece of Gulf front that's the only part them Jansons didn't buy."

"Are you mayor now, Judge?"

"Lord, boy, it's been a mighty long time since I was mayor. Or anything else. I was on the County Commissioners a while, but it like to kill me running over to all those meetings in Davis all the time. Seventy-one-mile round trip to argue about if we should buy a two-bit record book. I couldn't get no place political after Spence Larkin died. You know we were close, and just about anything he wanted to happen in this town, it happened. Anybody try to cross Spence and they'd find out he picked up their paper from the bank and he'd start in a-squeezing on them."

"When did he die, Judge?"

"Let me look back now a minute. Yes, that was in nineteen and fifty. Seems he had a gut pain he didn't pay enough attention to, and he finally went up to Tampa and they checked him over and said they wanted to operate. So he come back and he was busy as hell selling stuff and getting all his business stuff straightened away. And he went back up there and they operated and he up and died the next day. There was me and one or two others and his family that felt sorry about it, but the rest of the town went around sort of trying to hide a big grin. He was a man didn't give a damn for making himself popular."

"Did Jenna get down for the funeral?"

"Lordy, no. They never knew how to get hold of her fast. But she found out somehow and she was down here about two weeks later, storming around. Come in a great big car along with some funny-looking people. She'd done her hair red and she wore the tightest pants ever seen around here, son. Didn't even stay over the night. Just found out from her folks that the will said she was to get one dollar, so damn if she didn't go over there across the street to Wilson Willing's office and collect the dollar and take off. Buddy Larkin didn't make the funeral either. He was off there in Korea running up and down them hills with the marines. The only family here was Betty and her ma. Betty was seventeen then, thereabouts. Well, sir, old Angel Cobey, he was running the boat yard for the heirs, and when Buddy came back home it didn't take him long to find out Angel was stealing the family blind. Buddy brought a marine pal of his back, name of Johnny Geer. So they pitched in and they did fair with it, but they didn't begin to do real good until about fifty-four when Betty come home from college in Gainesville and pitched in too. Buddy is good on the mechanical end, but it's Betty's got more the head for business like Spence had. Of course their ma, Lila, she's got no more head for business than a water turkey. Spence had left the business awful run down. He wasn't interested in it. Now, Lordy, they get boats in there from all the way from Tarpon Springs to Marathon, boats where people want the work done right and done reasonable. They turned it into a corporation so Johnny Geer could get a piece of it, and they wrote Jenna to see if she wanted in and she said she didn't want no gifts."

"Judge, I'm a little confused on this thing. What for would they want to run that boat yard? After what Mr. Larkin must have left?"

"Well, I'll tell you what Spence left, son. He left that house on Grove Road all free and clear. And a thousand shares of bank stock you can't sell and hasn't paid a dividend in years. And a pretty good new Cadillac. You remember that was about the only thing he ever bought himself, a new car every year and run the living hell out of it. And about eleven thousand in cash. And the boat yard. Oh, and some little pieces of acreage. No-account land."

"Where did it all go anyhow?"

He chuckled. "Good question, son. The tax folks would like to know too. By God, you never saw such digging. Like to tore up half the county looking for Spence's money. Thought they were about to turn up an old coffee can with a million dollars in it. There's some kind of tax action been dragging along in the courts."

"Do you think he hid the money, Judge?"

"I know he had plenty that never showed up. The way I figure it, Spence wasn't quite ready. He counted on some more time. But he got cut off too quick. Son, it was one hell of a funeral. About half of Tallahassee down here, and folks out of county government from all over hell and gone. Ole Spence had put the screws to most of them and the word was they come to make sure he was really dead. When they lowered the box, you could dang near hear the big sigh of relief. Me, I liked old Spence, mean as he was. You just had to understand him. His daddy fished commercial all his life and when they buried him they bought a used suit coat and a new necktie. And borrowed the white shirt. Spence and me were a pair of raggedy-ass kids in those days, and that didn't bother me as much as it did him. It bothered him a lot. And so he spent his life correcting that state of affairs. And he was one hell of a lonely man the whole time. Seems like Jenna was the only thing really meant anything to him outside of the money. But she had that wildness in her. Got it from her grandma, Spence's mother, I'd say. That woman kicked up her heels all over three counties afore work and kids ground her down. And the only kid lived to grow up was Spence."

"And then Jenna came back for the second time," Alex said.

"She surely did. Just about a year and a half ago, with her important husband in such bad shape they had to ambulance him from Tampa airport all the way down here. She'd been down ahead of him and rented the old Proctor cottage out on the beach and fixed it up some, and then went back and got him. It had been in the *Davis Journal* about her marrying him, but you couldn't get folks around here to really believe it. But they believed it all right when she showed up, better than seven years after Spence passed away. Maybe she came back here to prove she'd done good. I don't know. But she come back a lady, son. In dress and talk and manners. You never hear such gabbling and cackling as the women did. Said she looked hard in the face, but I couldn't see it. She looked fine to me. Didn't mix much, not with him so sick, but she saw a lot of Betty and Buddy and her ma. She was nursing that colonel back to health. And she kept it up about six months."

"I saw some of the newspaper stuff when she was killed, Judge. It sort of hinted she'd been living it up."

"Out of the clear blue she shows up one night over there in the Spanish Mackerel on Front Street, Harry Bann's place. The Mack ain't changed since you were here, son. It's rough and tough most of the time, and gets worse when those people down to Bucket Bay come up to town to raise hell. So she had some drinks and she played the jook and the pinball and the bowling and didn't leave until the bar closed and then she didn't leave alone."

The judge winked ponderously and said, "There's a lot of fellas around here in their thirties and early forties that first learned what makes the world go round from Jenna. And the pride in any man says that if he's once bedded a woman he can do it again. And if it's been a long time, he gets an itch to prove he's the man he used to be. So while Jenna was being a lady, they were trying to edge in on her and getting no place at all. And when she stopped being a lady, they gathered around pawing the ground something fierce. It was like she stopped giving a damn. Find her in the Mack almost any night, sopping it up. Some army friend had drove their car down, a blue Olds, one of the small ones, and you could find it parked in front or out in that lot behind the place any time. Well, sir, after she got picked up for drunk driving, the colonel's sister come down to take care of him, and I don't guess Jenna and the sister got along so good. Buddy and Betty and Miz Larkin were trying to get Jenna straightened out again, but it was like the old days. She wouldn't listen to nothing. She drove the car after they took away her license and she racked it up for fair. Chopped down a big old cabbage palm with it. Total loss. Then she took to disappearing two and three days at a stretch. Come back hung over to rest up and start all over again.

"Well, sir, that went on until last November on the twenty-first day, a Friday. Better to call it Saturday morning, I guess. She was in the Mack from maybe eight o'clock on. I stopped in and saw her. Just happened to see her. Bright yella slacks and a little white sweater, but both of them looking slept in, and her hair tangly, and no money so people were buying her drinks for her. There was always somebody around to buy Jenna a drink. They say Buddy came in about eleven to get her to go home. She didn't have transportation. But she bad-mouthed him and he took off and left her there. But I guess you read all about it, son."

"I can't remember it so good."

"Near as anybody can tell she left the place alone to walk back. It would be a mile, or a little better. And it would make easier walking on the beach than on that

sand road. She left a little after two, and the one found
her on the beach at daybreak, halfway home, was that
crazy old Darcey woman that goes shelling at dawn
every day of her life no matter what weather it is. Jenna
was there, on her back, her head up the beach slope and
her feet in the water. No rape or anything like that.
Somebody had busted her a dandy on the jaw. It had
chipped her teeth. And then they'd took hold of her by
the throat and held on. I tell you it made one hell of a
sight for that Darcey woman to come up on. You know
something. She hasn't acted half as crazy since then, and
she hasn't been shelling one time.

"Well, sir, you never seen such a fuss as we had
around here. Sheriff Roy Lawlor, he come over from
Davis, and Parnell Lee, the State's Attorney, he was
here, and both of them acting like the one in charge.
And there was some kind of special investigator down
from Tallahassee. And we had reporters from as far
off as Atlanta. More questions asked and picture-taking
than you ever saw. For once the town was full up. They
questioned the colonel's sister and, when she finally let
them, the colonel, but they'd both gone to bed early
and anyway back then the colonel was still in no shape
to go around killing anybody, even a little bit of a thing
like Jenna. They questioned everybody lived on the
beach which wasn't many, and they locked up just about
every customer the Mack had had that night. I guess it
was all on account of that Colonel M'Gann being a sort
of national figure and Jenna having been, in a manner
of speaking, in show business. The papers really struggled
keeping that story alive. Some smart fella with a long
memory on a Miami paper, he dug around until he got
hold of one of those art photography magazines from way
back about forty-eight where dang near the whole issue
was pictures of Jenna, naked as an egg. And there
were a few of them you could just barely print in a
family newspaper, like one of her holding a big black

cat to kind of cut off the view. So those wire service people picked those up and as you know I guess there wasn't a man in the country didn't find out Jenna was built pretty good. You know, son, back when that magazine came out, while Spence was still alive, somebody from here found a copy on a stand over in Orlando, and he bought all they had and he went around and bought a lot more copies from other stands, and for a time there this town was full up with copies of that magazine. Then somebody sneaked one onto Spence's desk over to the boat yard and why he didn't fall over with a stroke I'll never know.

"Yes, sir, we had us a time last November. Cash registers ringing all over town. It's a wonder the junior chamber didn't try to set up a murder a week to keep things humming. The big shots just elbowed Donnie Capp out of the way. I don't know if you remember him. He got himself a little shot up in the service and got doctored out in forty and three, and when he came back, Sheriff Roy Lawlor he made Donnie a deputy and he's been that ever since. And Donnie takes care of this end of the county all by his own self. Knows every inch of it. He purely loves to beat heads. He had to sit way back while Lawlor and Lee were around here puffing out their chests.

"But they couldn't find out a thing and so it all kind of dwindled away. Jenna is planted right beside Spence. Wonder sometimes if they've had a chance to make up. Before she run off there was an outside chance Spence could have turned into a human being. But that tore the rag off the bush." He sighed. "You get an old man to talking, son, and you've got yourself an all-day listening job. What you been doing all the time you've been gone?"

"A couple of wars, Judge. And knocking around here and there. South America. Construction work. Decided maybe I'd come back and look around. Might settle here."

"Like I said, there's no future here. Not in Ramona. The young folks leave fast as they can. Town gets older every year. The waters are about fished out. All the cypress has been logged out. The deer and the turkey are all gone. We got some retireds moving in. Folks that like it quiet and ain't got much to do with. It's quiet all right. Always had the idea I'd like to see some of the world. The furthest away place I ever did get to was Chicago, in nineteen and twenty-six when we made up a committee and went up to dicker with those Janson folks about the land. Scared hell out of me up there."

"Judge, are you still in the real-estate business?"

"Not to strain me none. Got an office just around the corner on Gordon Street. Took a woman in with me, name of Myrtle Loveless. Got a lot of energy, Myrtle has. A Carolina woman that got her divorce down here and stayed on. She does most that has to be done."

"I think I'd like to rent a beach cottage."

"Good time to do it, son. Town folks don't move out there until school's over. Got a pretty good choice right now. You just go see Myrtle. Tell her you're a friend of mine."

"I . . . I guess people are going to remember what happened when I left."

"Sure they'll remember. There isn't enough happens here to cloud up their minds. Most kids do fool things. Some folks will try to nasty things up for you. Do you care?"

"I guess so, Judge."

"Nice to see you back home, son."

As Alex left Ducklin's, turning toward Gordon Street, he saw a young man walking toward him, a slouching, swaggering kid of about twenty-three or four with red hair worn too long, a pinched, insolent face boiled red by the sun, faded jeans patched at the knees, a soiled white sport shirt. When the blue eyes stared at him in reckless, arrogant appraisal, Doyle felt his muscles tighten with ancient angers. And just as suddenly he realized that this could not be Gil Kemmer. He was too young to be Gil. But he was one of the Kemmers. One of the wild breed from Bucket Bay.

The young man stopped in front of Alex and said, "Know you, don't I?" There was a sharp reek of raw corn.

"I used to know Gil pretty well. I'm Alex Doyle."

"I'll be damn. I'm Lee Kemmer. You and Gil used to pound on each other regular. You bust his wrist one time."

"He tried to cut me."

Lee Kemmer swayed in the sunlight, grinning in a knowing way. "Gil didn't get the breaks they give you, Doyle. He drew four at Raiford. He's been out a year, keeping his head down. He draws a little county time now and again on account of they pick on us Kemmers all the time. And need their damn road work done for free. This is a rough place for anybody likes a little fun. Let's you and me go to the Mack and drink up some beer, Doyle."

"Thanks. I've got things to do."

"You still too good for the Kemmers?"

"It isn't that."

"If my brother couldn't whip you, maybe I can. We'll try that some time. I'll tell Gil you're back in town."

Doyle shrugged and stepped around him. When he looked back, Lee was still standing there, grinning at him.

Alex walked to the real-estate office, a small place with a big window, a cluttered bulletin board, a wide hearty woman with black hair cut like a man's sitting on the corner of a desk talking over the phone. She cupped her hand over the phone and said, "Have yourself a chair. Be through here in a minute. Now, Emily Ann, you're jus' not bein' realistic, honey. No, I certainly don't want you to give the lot away, but after all, honey, you've had it on the market three years and this is the first firm offer that's come in, and I think it's better to take it than keep paying taxes on that little old lot. All right, I'll see if he'll come up just a little bitty bit more. And let you know. 'By, honey."

She hung up and said, "Her husband's been dead twenty years and he bought that lot for forty dollars and now she doesn't want to sell it for twelve hundred. I'm Myrtle Loveless. Can I help you?"

"Alex Doyle. The Judge says to see you about renting a beach cottage."

"I've got listings, but they're kinda on the primitive side, Mr. Doyle. They . . ."

"I used to live here. I know what they're like. I'd want one for a month."

She opened a big key rack. A half hour later he paid her eighty dollars for a one-month rental, picked up groceries at the supermarket without seeing anyone he knew, and drove back on out to the Carney cottage on the beach. It was of weatherbeaten cypress and sat two feet off the ground on thick piers. There was a small living room with rattan furniture and a grass rug, a bedroom, a small and primitive kitchen in the rear with a very noisy refrigerator, an inside bath with tub, and an outside cold-water shower. On the front was a small screened porch with two chairs of corroded aluminum tubing and plastic webbing. The front porch was fifty feet from the high-tide line. He stowed his supplies, took a long swim and a cold shower, and then sat on the screened porch with a cheese sandwich and a bottle of milk, squinting through the white glare of the sand toward the deep blue of the early afternoon Gulf.

The cottage on his left, visible beyond the trees, was empty. Myrtle had told him that the next cottage to the north was also empty. He could not see that one. Beyond that one was the Proctor cottage where Colonel Crawford M'Gann lived with his sister.

He realized that somehow the world had reverted to the dimensions of childhood. This was the known place. So well known. He and Jody Burch had gone gigging along this beach line in Jody's old scow, with a home-made tin reflector around the Coleman lantern, taking turns with the gig. Not two hundred yards from where he sat, but twenty years ago, he had helped work the nets when that unforgettable school of mullet had appeared, a mile and more of mullet, a hundred yards wide and five feet deep, almost solid enough to walk on. Hundreds upon hundreds of tons of fish, so that every boat had been out. And he had taken them out of the gill net until his arms had been like lead. But it hadn't done anybody any good. They'd been getting seven cents a pound, but it dropped to five and then three and then a penny, and then you couldn't get rid of them. And they had been buried under fruit trees and rose bushes all over town.

The Sunday school picnics had nearly always been at the Proctor cottage where the colonel was now living. And you showed off by swimming out as far as you dared, pretending not to hear the Reverend Mountainberry bellowing at you to come back.

Up the beach a little farther was where you and Ed Torrance set out all those stone crab traps that year and did so well. And the stone crabs bought that American Flyer bicycle, and Joe Ducklin got so sore because he thought the money should have gone for clothes.

A vivid world, every inch of it known. And now, as in childhood, the rest of the world did not exist, except as colored maps and faraway names. He had been out into a lot of that world, but now it did not seem real. It was like something he had made up. This was the home place, and the bright borders of it were those farthest places you had been when you were a kid. Beyond the borders was a hazy nothingness.

The Gulf was flat calm, the day strangely still—without thrash of bait fish, or tilting yawp of terns or the busy-legged sandpipers.

He heard, in the stillness, a distant rumbling of the timbers of the old wooden bridge, and the sound of a rough automotive engine, coming closer, running along the sand and shell road between the cottages and the bay shore. He heard it stop directly behind the cottage. He got up and walked back to the kitchen door and looked out through the screen and saw a battered blue jeep parked next to his old gray Dodge. A sign on the side of the jeep said, *The Larkin Boat Yard and Marina— Ramona, Florida.*

A girl had gotten out of the jeep. She stood for a moment, looking toward the cottage, and then came toward the back door.

chapter THREE

SHE WAS A GIRL of good size and considerable prettiness, and she came swinging toward him, moving well in her blue-jean shorts and a sleeveless red blouse with narrow white vertical stripes and battered blue canvas topsiders. She had been endowed with a hefty wilderness of coarse blond-red hair, now sun-streaked. She was magnificently tanned, but it was the tan of unthinking habitual exposure rather than a pool-side contrivance of oils and careful estimates of basting time.

She stopped at the foot of the two wooden steps and looked up at him through the screen, and smiled in a polite and distant way. There was, he thought, an interesting suggestion of the lioness about her face, the pale eyes spaced wide, a sloping heaviness of cheek structure, a wide and minutely savage mouth.

"I'm sorry to bother you."

"Doesn't bother me a bit. Come on in."

She came into the kitchen, a big, strong, vital-looking woman, and when she was on his level he knew that if she were to wear high heels, she would stand eye to eye with him.

"Myrtle should have remembered this. Mrs. Carney has been letting us use the cottage to change in when it isn't rented. And we left some stuff out here. Maybe you've run across it and wondered about it. Here's the extra key. I don't imagine you want a stranger having a key to your castle."

"Some castle. I haven't found anything. I haven't looked around much."

"Just some swimming gear in that little closet off the living room. Suits and fins and masks and towels. I ran into Myrtle on Bay Street and she said she'd just rented it. I'll get the stuff if it's all right."

"It isn't going to be in my way. I'm not going to use that closet. As far as I'm concerned, you can leave it right here and come on out with your husband and swim any time you feel like it."

"I come out with my brother. We couldn't impose on you that way, really."

And suddenly he knew the reason why she had seemed so curiously familiar to him. She was Jenna, cut from a bolder pattern. And more forthright than sensuous, more grave than mischievous. He wondered why he had been so slow to recognize the obvious.

"Aren't you Betty Larkin?"

"Yes, and I've seen you before. A long time ago. And I just can't remember. Myrtle didn't tell me your name."

"Doyle. Alex Doyle."

Her eyes widened and she lifted her hand to her throat. "Of course! Of course! And you haven't changed so terribly much. Golly, I had such a horrible crush on you, I don't see how I could have possibly forgotten." Her color deepened under her tan.

"This isn't flattering, Betty, but I just can't remember you at all. I knew Jenna, of course. And I can remember Buddy a little bit. But you're a blank."

"I used to go into Ducklin's and make a lemon dope last just about forever. But the big football hero wouldn't have had any time for eleven-year-olds. Oh, I was a living doll, Alex. Nearly as tall as I am now, and I looked like something made out of broomsticks. We went to all the home games and some of the out of town ones. Every time they wrote anything about you in the *Davis Journal,* I'd cut it out and paste it in a book. With appropriate comments in my diary. Isn't it crazy the things kids do?"

"It sure is. But I'm flattered anyhow."

"Have you been in town long?"

"Just since mid-morning. Haven't seen anybody to talk to except Judge Ellandon. Sat with him in Ducklin's and got a briefing on the local picture. I can't offer a lemon dope, but the beer I bought ought to have a chill on it by now."

"Sounds good. Right out of the can or bottle, please."

He opened two cans of beer and they took them out onto the small screened porch. She asked him what he'd been doing, and he told her just what he'd told the judge. And then, as though sensing what he'd most want to know, she began to talk of his friends. Who had married and who had died and who had moved away. Who had children and who had been divorced. Having an older brother and sister had given Betty a better working knowledge of his age group than she would otherwise have had. There were only a very few names he could recall that she could not tell him about.

He was astonished that so many of them had moved

away. When she started to tell him about Jody Burch he said, "I heard about that. Junie was in Ducklin's with a woman named Kathy Hubbard. She told me about Jody. It's a damn shame. And then, all of a sudden, she remembered the dirt about me. And got a little nasty and took off."

"Junie is a terrible pill, Alex. Too bad Billy Hillyard ever married her. She's full of virtue and civic works, but the truth is her home and her kids bore her. That's why she's on so many committees."

He said, into the sudden silence, "Well, when the big hero fell off the pedestal, it sure must have raised hell with your diary."

She grinned at him. It was a good grin that slanted her eyes and wrinkled the tan nose. "It blighted my life. I was your valiant defender, Alex. I got in more darn kicking, scratching, snarling, hair-yanking fights over you. I couldn't *bear* to have anybody call you names."

"But I guess they did."

"They certainly did. You were drinking and you weren't used to drinking, and you'd never been in trouble before. I couldn't understand why people were so . . . vicious about it."

"Don't you know, really?"

"No," she said, frowning.

"I was Bert Doyle's kid. A kid from Chaney's Bayou which was just about a half step better than Bucket Bay. I was from down there where they throw the trash and garbage off the front stoop into the bay, down there where they fish all week and get stinking drunk on Saturday night. My old man and my brother drowned in the Gulf and my old lady scrubbed in the kitchen at the Ramona Hotel until she died, and it was too damn bad Joe Ducklin had such no-account kin, but it wasn't really close kin, and wasn't Joe a hell of a fine man to take me in like he did? They never thought how much wages Joe saved. So I was supposed to be grateful and know my place. And it made them all uneasy when I got better grades than their sons and daughters, and they felt kind of strange about it when I could run harder and faster and carry a ball better than their sons. And get up quicker when I was hurt. And it didn't seem right I should be popular in school and get invited to things, and run around with their kids. I guess they'd look at me and see I was mannerly and knew which fork to use, and they wished they could put a big tag on me, saying I was bayou trash. I was too big for my britches. So then I did just what they wanted. I did it up fine. Got drunk and robbed good old Joe. That proved something, didn't it? You cain't trust that bayou trash. They'll turn on you ever' time. Got that mean shifty streak in 'em.''

He turned his head violently away from her and looked blindly south down the afternoon beach, and felt the unexpected sting of tears in his eyes.

"Oh, Alex, Alex," she said softly, and for just a moment she laid her hand on his arm, and took it away. "It was long ago. You were just a kid."

When he was sure of his control he turned back toward her and smiled a crooked smile. "It was so long ago, wasn't it, that there wouldn't be any point in my lying now?"

"I . . . I wouldn't think so. What do you mean?"

"The sad crazy thing about it is I didn't do it."

She was frowning, her eyes moving quickly as she searched his face. "But you pleaded guilty. It was in the papers."

"I pleaded guilty. They talked to me and talked to me and they said if I tried to fight it I'd end up in Raiford sure as hell. So be sensible, kid, and plead guilty and it's all set so the judge'll let it drop if you enlist right off. And I was going to enlist anyway. That was what the party was about. I passed out. Somebody took the store key out of my pocket and they went and they took twenty cartons of cigarettes, and those pens and lighters, and nearly two hundred dollars out of the register. Then they shoved the key and two twenty-dollar bills and three fountain pens in my pockets."

"But you *should* have fought!"

"I know that *now,* Betty. But I was sick and I was scared and I was confused. All I wanted was to get out of that cell and get in the army and never think about Ramona again."

"Why didn't you write Joe later and tell him the truth, Alex? Or write any of your friends?"

"I wouldn't have written Joe. I should have written to Myra. I must have started a dozen letters. I couldn't say it right. I tore them up. I told myself when I got out of the service I'd come back and clear things up. I was going to be my own private eye and find out who did it. But I got out and . . . I couldn't make myself come back. I knew I'd never come back."

"And now here you are."

"I got older. And smarter, maybe."

"But it still hurts, doesn't it? You sounded so bitter it made me feel . . . sort of strange. Have you thought of who could have done it?"

"It was a big party, Betty. A beer party and dance. I guess over a hundred of the kids. I kept having to make speeches. It was Willy Reiser brought that raw 'shine, and we got to drinking it out of paper cups. They let us have the Legion Hall and when I passed out early, they put me in one of those little back rooms and stuck flowers in my hand and went on with my going-away party. Almost anybody could have done it. It isn't a long walk from Ducklin's to the Hall. They'd need a car, maybe, to carry the cigarettes, but anybody who didn't have a car could borrow one. I'll never know who did it, Betty."

"What a filthy, filthy trick! Worse than the stealing was making it look like it was you. But even so, Joe wouldn't have had to swear out a complaint."

"Hell, he enjoyed it. Do you know something? Outside of trying to tell the county police fifteen years ago and Joe, you're the first person I've ever told this to? It became sort of a point of honor to keep it to myself. I guess I told you because . . . of the clippings and the diary and those scraps you had over me. Now tell me about yourself, Betty. I want to know about my fan club of one."

"I . . . I'm not the dramatic one in my family. I'm just a big healthy uncomplicated horse. After I got out of school in Gainesville I came back here and went to work in the yard. I'm sort of a top sergeant or general manager or something. Buddy bosses all the shop work and I take care of everything else. Buddy and I live with mother at the same old house on Grove Road. Johnny Geer rents a room from mother, and we pay our share of the board."

"Work, and go swimming?"

"And sailing, Alex. In my little Thistle. Called the *Lady Bird*. And that's about it. It's enough. We're all sort of trying to recover from . . . what happened."

"I'm very sorry about it, Betty."

She shrugged. "I guess something was going to happen to her. Nobody knew what it would be. But I do wish it hadn't been this. Somebody did it. They may be still around. Pretty spooky. Buddy and I have talked about her. I guess we loved her, but not very much. You can't love anybody who doesn't want love, who won't accept it." She looked at her watch. "I've goofed off too long."

"Come back, will you? Any time at all."

"Stop in and look at the yard."

"I will. And leave your gear here. It isn't in my way."

"Well . . . all right."

He walked out to the jeep with her. She turned and shook hands with him. Her hand was solid, her grip strong but feminine. "Hope you'll stay around a while, Alex."

"I hope so too."

"I guess you knew Jenna . . . pretty well."

It was a hesitant question and he saw a look of uneasiness, almost of pain, in her eyes before she looked away.

"We were in the same crowd, but I wasn't somebody special to her. Why?"

"I don't know. I was just talking."

"Did they find her very far from this cottage?"

She slid under the wheel and looked up at him. "You can ask questions, Alex, and they'll be answered because you're from Ramona. But it isn't a very healthy place for strangers who come around prying. It's all over and the town wants it to be forgotten. There was some very . . . strong meat written. At first the town was excited, but now it's kind of ashamed. We kept the worst of it away from mother, thank God. And I guess Celia kept Colonel M'Gann from seeing much of it. It wasn't far from this cottage, Alex. About three hundred yards south. Just opposite that stand of three big Australian pines."

"How is Colonel M'Gann taking it?"

"I wouldn't know. Celia wants no part of the Larkin family, and what Celia wants, Celia gets. Not one of us has seen the colonel since . . . it happened. And I guess that suits Celia perfectly. Her dear brother married so far beneath him. Sorry, but she makes me want to spit. See you later, Alex."

He watched the jeep until it went out of sight around a bend. At the last moment she looked back and waved. He was pleasured by the picture it made, the faded blue jeep and the spume of white shell dust behind it, and her vivid hair and the warm brown of shoulders and arms and the red of the blouse. As he reached the back door he heard the bridge timbers again after she turned on to the causeway.

He took another can of cool beer out on the porch and he wondered why he felt so utterly relaxed, felt such inner peace. And he decided that telling her the truth had been for him a kind of therapy he had not realized he needed so badly. It was like retching away something that had lain sour and heavy on his stomach. And he thought of the tall spindly child fighting so fiercely for him, and it made him smile.

There was such an odd contrast between Jenna and Betty in spite of the elusive resemblance. It had been almost impossible for Jenna to walk or move or speak without making of it an act of provocation. The fabric of her sexual tensions had surrounded her with an unmistakable aura of awareness and surmise.

Betty, in contrast, seemed to handle herself in a way that, through long habit, seemed to negate her bounties, to underplay her charms. She seemed to have no body awareness, no iota of consciousness of self. So there was a bluffness in the way she moved, an asexual indifference. It was a big lovely body, with good shoulders and strong breasts, delicately narrow waist, and long strong shapely legs. Yet when she had sat on the porch she had propped her heels on the railing just inside the screening, and crossed her ankles with neither coyness nor seemingly any awareness that she was good to look upon.

It gave him the feeling that should a man attempt to kiss her, it would surprise her utterly. And she would glare at him and say, with great impatience, "Oh, for heaven's sake!" So it was no wonder that at twenty-six she was unmarried, and seemed perfectly content with that condition.

He finished his beer and put on swim trunks and swam down the beach and came ashore at the stand of three tall pines. There was no mark or footstep on the sand where the tide had gone out. A tan crab ran sideways to its hole and popped in and watched him with stalked eyes. So she had been found just about here. And, with forlorn irony, on her back. In soiled white sweater and soiled yellow slacks, with damaged mouth and staring eyes and darkened face, black tongue parting the swollen lips.

He could remember her so clearly on another beach. Mouth that he had kissed. Eyes and throat that he had kissed.

A drunken little lady in her yellow slacks treading an uncertain path back along the night beach to where the invalid husband slept. Singing her small drunken songs in the night. Saying "Lay di ah" and "Doe di ah" in the parts where she couldn't remember the lyrics. Walking there, with someone coming along behind her, swiftly. Or waiting for her in the black pine shadows, perhaps hearing the drunky song first and then seeing the pallor of the sweater and slacks against the November night.

There was one other memory of Jenna that was especially vivid. There had been a beach picnic and swimming by moonlight, down near Windy Pass. And a big fire that burned down the coals. There was an improvised game, selecting weird, comic futures for each member of the group. Jenna sat in Buddha pose, a boy's jacket around her shoulders, the fire glow red on her face. The game had become more serious, with each person stating what they wanted to be. When it was Jenna's turn she had looked almost broodingly at the dying fire, a strangely quiet Jenna, all vivacity gone for the moment.

"I guess I just want to *be*. I don't want a choice, and be just one thing, one kind of person. I want *all* the choices." She had jumped up, thrown the jacket aside, shoved Willy Reiser over onto his back with her bare foot, then raced for the water, with Willy after her, yelling horrid threats.

Alex looked at the unmarked beach where they had found her, and suddenly he felt a queasy crawling of the skin at the nape of his neck and the backs of his hands. An atavistic warning. He looked up and down the beach, but it was empty. Only the tan crab watched him, wary and patient.

chapter FOUR

THE NEXT MORNING was sultry and misty, with an oily gray Gulf and a slow gentle swell that curled and slapped the packed sand. At dawn he had heard the rush and thrash of game fish striking bait just off the beach, and so later he had driven over into town to Bolley's Hardware and bought a cheap spinning outfit, and some white and yellow nylon dudes.

He was waited on by Cal Bolley, the son of the owner. Alex remembered Clem Bolley, the father, as a fat, sullen man, driven and harried by a neurotic wife with social ambitions. And he remembered Cal as a fat, shy boy, butt of cruel jokes. The shyness had congealed to sullenness.

"Hello, Cal."

"Hello, Doyle." No smile or offer of hand or flicker of response.

"Glad somebody recognized me."

"Heard you were back in town. Over on the beach."

"How's your father?"

"Had a stroke. Hasn't been out of bed for three years." For the first time there was a flick of expression on the doughy face, a faint shadow of satisfaction, of a smothered glee.

"Sorry to hear it. I want to get a spinning rod."

"Over here. It'll have to be cash, Doyle. I don't run a credit business."

"It will be cash."

He picked out what he wanted. Bolley deftly ran monofilament onto the reel spool, dropped the lures and swivels and leader into a small paper sack. On the

other side of the store a clerk was demonstrating a
floor fan to an old lady.

As Alex paid and received his change, he said, "You
sure as hell give me a big welcome, Cal. Thanks."

Cal Bolley stared at him. "Want I should hire a band?
I can't keep you people out of the store. I'll take your
money when you've got any. I don't have to stand
around and carry on a big conversation."

As Alex walked to the door he was conscious of
Bolley standing there, watching him, the piggy little eyes
remote and suspicious.

After he got behind the wheel, he knew that there
was something he had to do, and the longer he delayed
it the more difficult it would become. He forced himself
to drive to Palm Street. The old house had been painted
not long ago, but it was the same color, cream with dark
brown trim. He glanced up at the window which had
been the window to his room, and went onto the porch
and pushed the bell, stood looking through the screen
into the dim hallway. It could well be like the response he
had gotten from Cal. But this time it would hurt.

"I'm coming, I'm coming," he heard her say, and she
came down the hall in a faded print dress, wiping her
hands on her apron, a little sparrow of a woman with
white hair, sharp features, an air of timeless nervous
energy.

"Yes?" she said and looked up at him through the
screen, and quite suddenly her face broke, a shattering
of delicate ancient glass. And for the first time he
realized how lovely a girl Myra Ducklin must have
been. She fumbled the screen open and tugged at him
and pulled him into the hallway, and hugged him and
made broken sounds against his chest that finally turned
into an endless saying of his name. She pushed him
away and, holding his arms, looked up into his face,
trying through tears to smile at him in an accusing
and disciplinary way.

"You never wrote!" she said in a shaky voice. "You never did write me one letter, Alex!"

"I tried, Aunt Myra. Honest to God, I tried!"

"Now no cussin' in front of a church lady." She clung to his hands. "You turned into a man, Alex. I guess nobody could call you handsome and I guess you know that. But you've got a good face, Alex. It's a good strong face. Come in the sitting room. Oh, it's so good to see you! It's been so long. So terrible long."

They went into the small, immaculate, old-fashioned parlor. She sat beside him on the couch and held his hand tightly and said, "There's a big box in the attic. I packed it all up. The old papers and things from your folks and the photographs and all. And your school records and those sports things you won, and the clothes you left behind. I put moth crystals in. Everything is safe, but I guess it wasn't much point, saving the clothes. Joe, he was going to throw everything out he was that mad, but I knew that wouldn't be a Christian act."

"I . . . I didn't have any idea you'd be so glad to see me, Aunt Myra. I guess Joe wouldn't have. I'm sorry about Joe."

"You just don't have much sense, Alex Doyle. That little trouble you had doesn't have anything to do with love, and you should know that. When there's love, the least you can do is give folks a chance to forgive, and you never even gave me a chance to go through the motions. I prayed for so long you'd come back, come to the door just like you did, and then I thought it would never happen and I guess I gave up praying. But there hasn't been a day in all that time I haven't thought about you and where you were and what you were doing. I'll tell you, I loved Joe Ducklin every day of my life, but the way he carried on about you and getting them to arrest you and all, it was pretty hard to keep on loving. Somehow . . . after that happened, it wasn't really ever the same between us. It was almost the same, but there was a little something gone. And that somehow made it worse when he died, Alex. I don't know why but it did."

"You make me ashamed of myself, Aunt Myra."

"Now let's not get carrying on, boy. I can see how you were terrible hurt, the way Joe did you. And a wife has to share the way people think about her husband. You did a real foolish thing and it looked like it was a mean thing, but I knew better on account I knew there was no meanness in you. It was strong drink that did it, and bad company. There was a wild bunch of young folk back then, and I can tell you they seem to get wilder every year, so you don't know what the world is coming to, and sometimes I think it will take one of those terrible bombs to make things clean again, but that is blasphemous talk. You just make it up now by telling me everything you've done in all the years you've been gone, Alex. I got to keep holding onto your hand to keep making sure you're here."

"Aunt Myra, I wasn't going to tell you this. But now I guess I should." She listened intently while he told her, just as he had told Betty Larkin, about the robbery.

When he was through she bobbed her head and she said, "Oh, if I could just be sure Joe Ducklin could know about this!"

"I tried to tell him, Aunt Myra, over in the jail in Davis, but he didn't feel like listening."

She looked surprisingly fierce for a moment. "He wouldn't let me go with him. And he never said a word about that. Not even on his dying bed did he have the . . . common decency to tell me anything about that. All I knew was you said you did it, boy, and they let you pick the army instead of jail. Well, it's all over now, but when you think on it, isn't it a terrible waste, boy? The things folks do to one another. I didn't even ask you if you're married!"

"I'm not married, Aunt Myra."

"That's no kind of life, Alex. Bad hours and bad food, and you turn into a fussy old bachelor. There's some nice girls right here in town."

"Don't go so fast!"

"Now you tell me what you've been doing."

He told her about the two wars, and far places. A young Negro woman, slim and pretty in a white uniform, came to the doorway and said nervously, "Miz Ducklin, I don't want to bust in, but that Miz Stimson, she don't look right to me. She breathing awful funny."

"Excuse me, Alex," Myra Ducklin said. She trotted off and he saw her hurrying up the hall staircase. She came down in a few moments and he heard her on the phone, apparently talking to a Dr. Kearnie, a name Alex did not recognize. She went back upstairs and was gone about ten minutes. The door buzzer sounded and the Negro girl admitted a young man with a medical satchel and a bold, unkempt black mustache.

A little later the doctor came down and used the phone and left. Myra came back into the parlor, looking tired and subdued.

"She died right after Dr. Kearnie got here. Old Mrs. Stimson. Ninety-one, she was. I won't be able to visit now, Alex. I got to phone the family, and then Jeffry Brothers will be sending over to pick her up. And then I'll have to visit with the other people I've got and cheer them up. They get awful low when somebody passes on."

"I don't understand, Aunt Myra. Is this a nursing home?"

"Licensed and everything," she said, and looked slightly ashamed. Ever since he had entered the house he had been subconsciously disturbed by the elusive and unfamiliar odor of medication and that sick sweet undertone of illness.

"When Joe passed on, if I'd had any sense, I'd have sold out the store right away. But I tried to run it myself and I didn't know as much as I thought I knew. So by the time I'd put most of the other money Joe left into it, I ended up having to sell it for less than I could have got in the first place. I like to keep busy. You know that. I've got two full-time girls to help with the cleaning and cooking and all, and one practical nurse, but she's off sick right now." She sighed, lowered her voice. "I know when I look at it square they're here to die, but sometimes it takes a lot of getting used to. Where are you staying, Alex? I can't even offer you a room. I turned that storeroom off behind the pantry into my bedroom. You aren't going to take off right soon again, are you?"

He told her he was out on the beach, and he was staying for a time. She kissed him and beamed upon him and patted his shoulder, her eyes shiny. "You came back, finally. I guess I knew you would all along. You'll have to come get that box of your stuff, boy."

Doyle drove slowly back out to the beach. Now that he had seen her, he wondered how he could have been so wrong in his thinking about her for so many years. It had been pride, perhaps, that corrosive disease, which had prevented him from seeing the truth his heart was trying to tell him.

He changed to trunks and assembled the rod and walked out onto the beach. Something was feeding noisily about two hundred feet out. He waded until the water was above his waist and, after a half dozen attempts, he was able to put the lure where he wanted it. It was a pearly day with a look of mystery, and he could feel the heat of the hidden sun. It was a school of four-pound jacks, wolfing the demoralized minnows. He beached four and released them before the school broke off feeding. The physical contest eased his emotional turmoil, his deep sense of guilt. It was nearly noon when, after a hundred glances north along the beach, he saw someone on the beach in front of the Proctor cottage. And, in what he hoped was a casual way, he began to move up the beach, casting aimlessly.

The woman squatted on the wet sand, right at the surf line. She had an aluminum pot and she seemed to be grubbing in the sand with her hands. He realized that she was digging up coquinas, those tiny brightly patterned clams that can be found an inch or so beneath the surface of the wet sand on nearly all the Gulf beaches.

She was very sun-browned, a trim-bodied, good-sized woman in a blue two-piece swim suit in batik pattern. She had hair that had grayed almost to white, cropped short. The muscles moved smoothly in her arms and shoulders as she searched for the coquinas, and she sat on her heels without strain.

She seemed to be unaware of him. He moved to within ten feet of her while retrieving a cast, and then said, "Pardon me, ma'am."

She looked up at him with obvious irritation. Her brows were heavy and jet black, her face angular, handsome. "Yes?" The voice was deep and rather husky.

"If you want to get those easy, you get you a piece of screen like they use sifting aggregate for concrete. You get a frame and props for it, and a shovel. And then you shovel that soupy sand against it and you'll get all the coquinas you can use."

"Thank you so much for your advice. I am not terribly interested in efficiency or speed. I prefer doing it this way."

"Okay, ma'am. Sorry. They sure make a wonderful broth, you just simmer 'em long enough. Me, I like it best real cold with a little Worcestershire and tabasco."

She returned to her task and did not answer. He cast again and retrieved the lure. "You must be staying here in the Proctor place, ma'am. Used to come here years back for Sunday school picnics. Miz Proctor, she was in charge of the whole Sunday school."

She looked up at him with exasperation. "That's all mildly interesting, I suppose, but I really don't feel . . . chatty."

"Just being neighborly. I'm two cottages down. Moved in yesterday. Name is Doyle. Alexander Doyle. Alex. Used to live here and I just came on back to see how the old place looks. Got homesick, I guess. First time in the States in three years. Down in Venezuela on construction jobs."

Her face darkened under the tan. "You don't seem to take a hint, Mr. Doyle. I understand that I can't order you off this beach, at least that area below the high-tide line. I would if I could. I do not feel like talking to you. I do not feel like giving you the opportunity to work the conversation around to the point where you can indulge your idle curiosity by asking dull questions about the colonel."

"Excuse me, ma'am, but I don't know what the hell you're talking about. What colonel? I'm not curious about anything. I wasn't working around to anything. I was just being friendly."

She stood up, facing him. From her face he guessed she was in the middle forties. She had the body of a far younger woman. "This cottage is where Colonel M'Gann lives. I am his sister. Does that name mean anything to you?"

"Why, sure! It does now. I knew Jenna Larkin in high school. I missed the papers, being out of the country like I was, but folks here have told me about it. Honest, I didn't know you people were in the Proctor place."

"In that case, Mr. Doyle, I want you to accept my apology for being rude. We have both had a . . . bellyful of magazine people and would-be writers and amateur detectives and plain curiosity seekers. So we have become rather . . . antisocial. The traffic has dropped off considerably, but we still get a few—one tiresome little man just last week who had the gall to want to see the colonel to ask him if he could ghost write a book for my brother. I chased him away and he became quite abusive. Horrible teenagers have walked here on the beach, pretending to choke each other and fall dead."

"Then if I was you, I'd move away. You're just renting the place, aren't you? Or did you buy it?"

"We're renting it, and your suggestion is most valid. I would dearly love to move away from here. But the colonel insists on staying."

"I'm not curious. Well, to be honest, I guess I am, a little. Anybody would be, naturally. But I don't care enough about it to come around asking questions. I guess it was a bad thing for you people but the way I look at it, unless that Jenna Larkin changed a hell of a lot since when I knew her, I guess she wasn't what you'd call a big loss. Hope I haven't said the wrong thing."

"You haven't, Mr. Doyle. Indeed you haven't! If any human being could be classified as worthless, Jenna could. And it is a terrible waste for my brother to keep on brooding about her. I hope I wasn't too rude to you."

"I don't mind. I understand how you'd feel about people trying to strike up a conversation. As long as I'll be a neighbor for a while, I just won't talk about it to you at all."

"That will be splendid, Mr. Doyle. You're one of the few sympathetic people I've found in this . . . truly dreadful community. They seem more like animals down here than people, really. I don't mean to offend you, of course."

"I guess it's because there isn't much goes on here, and when something does, they like to make a big thing about it."

Suddenly the gray surface of the water was torn and boiled just fifty feet away, and the small bait fish leaped in panic from predatory jaws. He cast beyond the area, yanked the dude into it, and felt the strike. He brought in a Spanish mackerel of about two and a half pounds.

He tossed it up on the beach and caught two more of the same size before the disturbance was over.

"Welcome to two of those if you can use 'em," Alex said. "One will do me. Mackerel. Good eating. They don't so often work in this close."

"You got them so quickly!"

"When they're working, you get them quick."

"Can I see that thing they bit on?" He held the lure so she could inspect it. "I will take the fish, and thank you very much, Mr. Doyle." She looked at him dubiously, uncertainly. "I . . . I wonder if you would do me a great favor, Mr. Doyle."

"Anything I can, ma'am."

"I have been trying to get my brother to take an interest in something. I thought fishing might be good for him. Neither of us knows anything about it. I bought a pole and things, and we fished with frozen shrimp, but it was all very boring. We got some nasty little catfish, and one horrible looking flat thing, and some little things with prickers all over them. But what you were doing looks as if my brother might enjoy it. The pole and reel I bought are much, much heavier than that thing you use. Is it hard to use?"

"No ma'am. It's easy."

"And it wouldn't be a . . . physical strain, I mean to catch something big?"

"Anything too big will just bust loose."

"If I give you the money, could you buy the same sort of outfit for the colonel? How much would it cost?"

"Less than twenty dollars for all he'll need. I can get it and you can pay me later when I bring it around."

"Well . . . all right. And then could you show my brother how to operate it? I don't really know if he *will* take any interest in it, but he does need some hobby. You see, he's never really had a hobby. Except all those model airplanes when we were little. I used to help him. We're twins. Then, when he was in school he worked. We both did. He didn't work when he was at the Point, of course. He has always been such a . . . dedicated man. So diligent. There was no room in his life for the things other men did. The fishing and the sports. Oh, he always kept himself in wonderful physical condition through exercise, so he could better accomplish his work. I sometimes wish he'd had more . . . desire and opportunity to play. Then maybe he wouldn't have been so vulnerable when she . . . Anyway, now that he can't work he has nothing to fill his time. I don't want to trouble you, Mr. Doyle, but I would . . . be most grateful to you."

"Glad to do it," he said.

"If you could find time to come around tomorrow with the fishing things? About this same time. He naps in the afternoon."

She thanked him again and put the two mackerel in the aluminum pot on top of the coquinas, the long slim mackerel tails protruding over the rim, rigid in death. He walked back toward the cottage with the single fish. Thus far it was all too easy. And would continue to be easy, very probably. It sometimes seemed terrifying to him that it was so utterly easy to disarm people by lying to them. People seemed so recklessly anxious to take you at your face value. They would believe what they wanted to believe, and you need only to guide their thinking in a gentle and unobtrusive way. It had worked so many times before, and it would work again. The fishing had been a lucky accident. But if it had not been the fishing, it would be something else. Celia M'Gann was obviously lonely. Once her suspicions had been quieted, she would have responded to casual friendliness. And, inevitably, he would have met the colonel. And, inevitably, made the chance to be alone with him. This fishing gambit did not alter anything. It merely accelerated things.

He cleaned and fried the mackerel and ate it for lunch. He thought of going in to see the Larkin boat yard. And see Betty again. But it seemed too soon. He had accomplished one decisive step in the mission. And now it was waiting time until he could walk up the beach tomorrow with the new tackle.

He stretched out on the bed and wondered who had taken over in Montevideo. He hoped they'd picked Schmidt. He wouldn't mess it up the way some of the new kids might. . . .

He came up out of sleep and heard somebody rapping sharply and insistently on the back door.

chapter FIVE

There was a sedan in the back yard, a dark dusty green with bumper aerial for short wave, and a red spot on the roof, and a faded yellow decal on the door that said *Sheriff—Ramona County*.

A man stood on the back steps, a dark silhouette against the white shell glare of the back yard. Doyle had belted on his old seersucker robe. He felt sweaty and fogged by sleep.

"I was sleeping," he said.

"So wake up," the man said, and pulled the door open and came into the kitchen. He was about five seven, with a toughened leanness about him, a deeply seamed and sallow face, narrow eyes the color of spit. He wore bleached khakis, tailored to his body and freshly pressed, a pale, cream-colored ranch hat. The trouser legs were neatly bloused over black gleaming paratrooper boots in a small and curiously dainty size.

On the pocket of his shirt was pinned one of the most

ornate badges Doyle had ever seen, large and golden, with some red enamel and some blue enamel. In a very legible way it said *Sheriff*, and in much smaller letters it said *Deputy*, and it said *Ramona County, State of Florida*, and bore some sort of ornate seal. He wore a black pistol belt with a black speed holster, old leather, shiny and supple with care and age, worn canted to bring the revolver butt-down to the level of "Gunsmoke." A chrome whistle chain disappeared into the other shirt pocket. A black night stick hung from the other side of the pistol belt, white leather thong suspended from a small brass hook.

He brought into the kitchen the slow creak and jingle of petty authority, and a thinly acid edge of sweat, a back-swamp accent and an air of mocking silence. Doyle felt irritated by his own feeling of intense wariness. It was a legacy from the faraway years when there would be trouble and men like this one would come to the bayou and go to Bucket Bay. You let them swagger through the house and poke around as they pleased. You never told them anything. And you never made a fuss because they would put knots on your head.

Yet on another level he sensed his kinship to this man. That light-eyed cracker sallowness, the generations of bad diet and inbreeding behind both of them that had resulted, curiously, in a dogged and enduring toughness, a fibrous talent for survival.

"I've seen you before," Alex said.

"Sure you've seen me before, Doyle. Turkey Kimbroy and I, we tooken you over to Davis long time ago to he'p you get in the army. If'n they'd shot your ass off, you wouldn't be back here giving me problems."

"I'm not making any problems."

"That's what I got to be sure about. Turkey don't have no problems any more. Fool nigger had a razor hung down his back and when Turkey beat on him a little, nig-

ger took one swipe and spilled Turk all over the side of
the road. Made me a carefuller man."

Doyle remembered how this Donnie Capp had been on
that long-ago ride, a pale slim blond man with a limp, not
afraid to be friendly to the boy they were taking in.

"What's that got to do with me, Donnie?"

The thin mouth tightened. "I get called Donnie by my
friends. Niggers and thieves, they call me Mister Deputy,
sir. You try it."

"Mister Deputy, sir."

"That's nice. Now stand still a minute. Okay. Now you
just walk on ahead of me slow while I look around some."

Capp made a leisurely and careful inspection of the cottage. He found the money belt on a hook in the back of
the bedroom closet. Doyle made no protest as he took it
out and unzippered it, fingered the money.

"Maybe you better come along in and tell Sheriff Roy
how come you got all the cash money, Doyle."

"If you think it's necessary, I'd be glad to."

"Then you can tell me how you got it."

"You can look in the top bureau drawer on the left
again, Mister Deputy, sir. Under the shorts. A folder with
passport and visas and work papers and pay vouchers."

He opened the folder, looked at the papers, threw
folder and papers on the bed.

"But right now you got no job, right?"

"No job. Not yet."

"Where do you figure on working?"

"Some place around here."

"I don't figure that way. I don't figure that way *at* all.
Over in Davis we got pictures of you and we got prints
and they're in a file. And that there is what you call a
dead file. Now I don't want to have to go move that file
up into the other file, the one where we keep the records
of people living around here. I'm just lazy, I guess. You
know, maybe you forgot to stop by and register as a
known criminal, Doyle?"

"Would that be necessary? It was a suspended sentence."

"I'm not up on all my law, but maybe it would have been sort of friendly of you to stop by when you come in and not let me find you by accident. And you could have brought us up to date on the police trouble you've had since you been gone."

"There hasn't been any."

"Guess you been clever about it, huh?"

"Can I ask you a question?"

"Always glad to oblige."

"Why are you on my back? I'm not in any trouble. I don't intend to get into any. I came back here because . . . this is home. That's all. There isn't any law about that, is there?"

"You know, Doyle, the end of this here county is about the cleanest end of any county in the state. Roy likes for me to handle it just the way I do, on account of he doesn't like sending in bad figures on crime up to Tallahassee. And he knows I know this end of the county better than anybody, so he just rides along and he lets me handle it all my own sweet way. You understand?"

"I guess so."

"And one way I do, anybody making for trouble, I just up and run 'em off. Let 'em light some other place. Let 'em go spoil the crime figures in some other county. Now if there's a family or something concerned, then I let 'em stay. But I persuade them to stay out of trouble. You haven't even got a job, so it's no trouble to run you off. Besides, I don't like having you out here on the beach. You stay down in Bucket Bay, I might think on letting you stay 'round."

"I want to stay right here."

"What you want and what you get is two different ends of the rabbit. All this here for miles around is my little ole bait bucket. I keep it nice and clean and throw out the spoiled bait. It isn't good for a fella like you not to

have a job. You lay around and get ideas and pretty
soon you make me some trouble. But I'll show you I'm
not a bad guy, Doyle. You paid a month rent, and it
ain't likely you can get it back. So all you got to do is
ask me nice if you can stay here, and tell me you won't
make trouble."

"I'd like to stay. Please. And I won't make trouble."

Donnie Capp smiled in a thin way and unhooked the
night stick, and glided toward Doyle. "Now I'll be quietin'
you down a little."

Just as Doyle started to back away, raising his arms,
the stick smashed down on the point of his left shoulder,
bruising the nerves, numbing his arm from shoulder to
fingertips. In painful reflex, he struck out at Capp with
his right fist. Capp stepped aside and paralyzed his right
arm with the same cruel and scientific blow, then shouldered him back against the wall beside the bedroom doorway. He could not raise either arm.

Capp jabbed the end of the club into the pit of Doyle's
belly, doubling him over. And then, calmly, professionally,
he went to work. Through the haze of pain and confu-
sion of impact, Doyle realized that he was getting a scientific head beating. No blow was enough to destroy consciousness. And, in between the rhythms of the blows
on his skull, Capp was taking practiced strokes at shins
and thighs, forearms and biceps, hips and calves. And, in
one area of cold and special horror, Doyle realized that
the man was crooning softly along with his grunts of exer-
tion. "Now . . . a little of this . . . and some more . . . of
that. And a touch here . . . and here."

He was only partially aware of it when Capp straightened him up and belted him across the belly and rib cage.
He swung one almost gentle blow into the groin, and
Doyle heard his own hoarse yell, coming from an echoing, metallic distance. He doubled, took a harder blow
than any of the others, directly over the ear, and tumbled
forward, sensing the impact of hitting the floor, but feel-

ing no pain from it. He lay on his side, knees against his chest, in a welcome silence.

With his eyes half open he could see the shiny black boots six inches from his face. Capp was somewhere above him, a thousand feet tall, talking to him in a remote voice.

". . . have the miz'ries for a couple days, Doyle. But you'll keep thinking on this long after you're walking real good. And you'll be nice and tame. On account of you know you make any trouble for Donnie Capp and he'll come back and we'll try it again, with a lot of different tricks I didn't even use. And we'll keep practicin' on it 'til we get it down perfect enough for television. Why, there's niggers I ain't laid this stick on in years, and all I got to do is show it to them and they turn white as a piece of soap. I want every time you think of Donnie Capp, you get sweaty. Then you'll be real good and safe to be around decent folk."

He saw the boots turn, and he heard the footsteps as Donnie went through the cottage. He heard the screen door slap shut, and then a car door, and then the explosive roar of a powerful motor. The motor sound died away.

He sobbed once, more in shame and anger than in pain. After a long time he began to slowly uncoil, straightening his body an inch at a time, enduring the agony. He rolled over onto his face, worked himself up onto his elbows and was wrenchingly ill. And then, like a half-trampled bug, he crawled a hundred miles to his bed. When he had rested long enough, he could pull himself up onto his knees and from that position squirm onto the bed. The effort exhausted him. There was a roaring in his ears. He turned and groaned and at last found the least agonizing position. And knew he could not sleep. And slid away then, sweaty, into sleep . . .

A moist and wonderful coolness on his forehead awakened him to a world where the face of Betty Larkin was close to his, vast and out of focus, her mouth angry and her eyes concerned as she held the cold cloth against his forehead. He became aware that it was a late afternoon world of slanting sun, and aware that his body was one vast throbbing, shimmering pain.

"I didn't get the license number," he said in a low and rusty voice.

"Do you feel awful?"

"I've never felt worse. Nobody has ever felt worse."

"I phoned Gil Kearnie to come out here too, and he ought to be along soon. Dr. Kearnie. He's new here and very good."

"How did you know about this?"

"I heard Donnie Capp talking to Buddy near the office. I just caught a few words and Donnie was talking about something he'd done to you. I know Donnie, so I went out and demanded to know. He said it wasn't any business of a nice girl like me, but he had heard you had come back so he'd come out here and got you quieted down. I said I didn't know you were excited. Then Buddy laughed at me and said that Donnie had just given you a little taste of the Ramona massage. So I called Donnie a dirty, sadistic little monster and I drove right out here. You didn't answer so I came in. And you looked so terrible, I hurried back and phoned Gil and came back here. He should be here any minute. I could kill Buddy for acting like he thought it was funny for Donnie to come here and hit you."

"It's an old southren custom, Miss Betty. Head beating. I can be thankful it was by an expert. It's the amateurs who kill you."

When Dr. Kearnie arrived, Betty let him in and went out into the other room while Dr. Kearnie examined him. Except for the mustache and the tired wise look around his eyes, Kearnie looked eighteen.

After poking and prodding, Kearnie dressed the two

places on Alex's skull and the one place on his left shin where the club had split the skin.

"He didn't hit you across the kidneys?"

"Not that I can remember."

"Good. That will save you a lot of pain. And that's dangerous. In some cases he's done some permanent damage."

"You've treated other . . . victims, Doctor?"

"A few. He's an expert. He's had years of practice, and he enjoys his work. I don't think there's any need of X-ray in your case. The ribs feel firm. If there's continuing pain, come on in to the office. You're in good shape, Mr. Doyle. If you have to take a beating, it helps to be in condition. I'll leave you something for pain. You'll feel a hundred years old tomorrow. My advice is force yourself to move around. Get out in the sun. Swim. Bake it out."

"And forget it?"

Kearnie raised one evebrow. "That wouldn't come under the heading of medical advice. But I don't believe it would be . . . practical to try to do anything about it. Not without several witnesses who can be kept beyond the reach of the deputy and his club. He's a psychopathic personality."

"How about the bill?"

"Drop in at the office. The nurse will have it. Take one of these every four hours. Two, if the pain is severe." He snapped his bag shut and stood up and for a moment ceased to be the formal and professional young doctor. "The psychological effects of a ·beating are interesting, Mr. Doyle. The standard result is a great big desire to keep your head down so it won't be whipped again."

"I think that's what he had in mind. Then I'm an exception."

"What's your reaction?"

"I'm going to fix his wagon, Doctor. I don't know how. I just want him one time, without that gun and club."

"I hope you get him. It would be a pleasure to have to patch him up."

After Kearnie left, Betty came back in and said, "Isn't he a lamb?"

"A nice little guy."

"What can I do?"

"I'd like some water so I can take one of those things he left, because I am hurting slightly fierce. And then if I can lean on you, I'd like to make it to the plumbing section. When I'm back in bed you can take off."

"No food?"

"I don't think so."

"And I think you will." She got water and he took the pill. He got his legs over the side of the bed and she pulled him to his feet with slow and gentle strength. He got his left arm around her shoulders. His arm felt like a big sausage roll full of putty. She put her brown right arm around his waist. She walked him slowly to the bathroom, helped him in, closed the door on him. When he came out he opened the door himself and took two teetering steps before she could hurry to him to support him. She told him he was the color of a sheet of paper, and helped him into bed. She brought his cigarettes, found more pillows and propped him up. He sat and smoked and inventoried his bruised areas, and listened with a certain domestic pleasure to the busy sounds she was making in the kitchen.

And thought, almost with calmness, about Donnie Capp. Those men had their uses. There had been a couple like that, ones he had been glad to take on patrol whenever he could. The catlike, fearless ones, the killing breed, amoral, antisocial, and entirely dangerous.

She had found a tray somewhere and she set it on a table she had placed close to the bed. The servings were abundant and smelled good, and he discovered that he was indeed hungry.

"You knew what you were doing out there, Miss Betty."

"That is one primitive kitchen. I guess I like to cook because I just live to eat. I eat like a wolf and never gain a pound. Knock wood. I am just not the dainty feminine type, I guess."

"You must have left work early."

"I'm my own boss down there, Alex. I'm pretty well caught up. Some delinquent accounts to needle. The slack season is starting. It will pick up a little in July, and then September will be a graveyard. When we're rushed, I'm one busy kid. I even pitch in on the other end when it's needed. I can clean and adjust a marine carb, adjust spark plugs, do compass compensation. And I can paint hell out of a hull."

"A paragon."

"Irreplaceable. Anyway, I like it. Sails and stinkpots both. The smell of marine varnish. Everything about the water. Buddy is the same way. We're hooked, I guess. We're on the stuff."

"To get back to Donnie Capp."

"Do we want to?"

"That little horror with the black club tried to turn me into a rabbit. The so-called nice people in Ramona don't mind having him around because he never whips their heads. Maybe they even think he's doing a good job. A man like that can be dangerous, Betty. He can get to thinking there's nothing he can't get away with."

"I guess I'm . . . guilty too, Alex. I'd heard how he likes to use that club, but I thought he used it on . . . people who needed it. I didn't know he'd do anything like this. Did you try to . . . throw him out or anything?"

"No. I know the type. He wanted the 'Mister Deputy, sir,' treatment and I gave it to him. To make sure I'd stay humble, he took his little club and went to work like a man felling a tree."

"That's terrible!"

"The worst thing is I can talk rough, but I know damn well I'd better not be fool enough to go after him."

"Well, I'll tell you one thing, Alex Doyle. He's not coming after you again. Even though Daddy's dead, there's still some push behind the name of Larkin. And I am going to let Donnie know and let Sheriff Lawlor know that if there's anything else like this, Buddy and I are going to make the biggest stink they ever ran into. And I know that doesn't change the fact that he has already hurt you."

"I've been hurt before. I'll get over it. But it would be nice to know it isn't likely to happen again very soon."

She took the tray away and washed the dishes and came back and sat by the bed. It was one of those rare evenings when for a short time all the world is suffused with an orange-yellow glow and all objects are strangely vivid and distinct. The glow from the window by the bed fell softly on her face, lighting it so clearly that he could see, in the light gray iris of her eye, little flecks of golden brown close to the pupil. And the strong brown column of her throat with the tender hollow at the base of it, and a heaviness of the level mouth, and a tawny brown of her eyebrows, a shade darker than the sun-struck mane of hair. Here was the special and stirring beauty of the female creature in perfect health, all glow and warmth.

She looked away suddenly and stood up with an awkwardness she had not displayed before. He knew he had stared at her too intently, and had upset her perfectly unconscious poise.

"I guess I'd better go."

"Thanks for everything you've done."

"It doesn't make much of a welcome home."

"I didn't expect too much."

"Alex . . . Just why did you come back?"

"I told you."

She looked down at him, frowning in the fading light. "Something bothers me a little. You don't seem to . . . fit."

"I don't know what you mean."

"Neither do I, exactly. Maybe I shouldn't try to say anything."

"Go ahead."

"You say you've been just wandering, working on construction jobs. The way you talk, it isn't always the same. Sometimes it's real piny woods talk. And then you change and talk as if you had a lot more . . . background and education. I'm not a snob. It just seems strange to me. And there is about you something I can't quite put my finger on. I guess it's sort of an unconscious . . . air of importance. Not importance, maybe. Significance. As if people had been paying attention when you had something to say. And those real sharp bright sports shirts and slacks don't seem to me to be . . . right. They're what you'd buy, I guess, if you are what you say you are. But in some way they're wrong for you."

"I'm bugged by the gay threads, doll."

"I just want to know if you're putting on some kind of an act that I don't understand."

"That's a pretty strange idea, Betty."

"Your nails are well kept, Alex. And your hands aren't callused."

"Nowadays we sit up there in those big cabs and push the little buttons."

"If it is an act, Alex, has it got anything at all to do with . . . Jenna?"

"Honey, I came back to my home town. With a buck or two saved. Thought I might stay if I found something just right. But the man worked me over good with his little club, and now I'm not so high on sticking around. When the lumps are gone, I might just up and move along in case he gets some more ideas. That's all there is."

She stared at him for a few more moments and then smiled and said, "All right. Good night, Alex."

He lay and listened to the jeep drive away into the dusk. He had a new and special appreciation for her. She was a big healthy blonde and he had been careless. Her

intuitions and perceptions were almost frighteningly keen.
There was nothing opaque about Miss Betty. And now
he could not, when he was with her, revert to a flawless
performance of the role he had selected for himself. She
was sharp enough to realize that would confirm her guess.
And so he would have to maintain the same level of
carelessness. It would be easier and safer to avoid her.
But he found that prospect surprisingly distasteful.

chapter SIX

By the time Doyle was up and shaved and dressed on
Thursday, he knew that it wasn't going to be one of
the best days he had ever spent. His arms were leaden.
Each slow movement had to be tested cautiously to see
how much it was going to hurt. Even in areas where he
could not remember being hit, his muscles felt as though
they had been dipped in cement and rolled in broken
glass.

It was a day of high, white, scattered clouds that fre-
quently masked the sun, and a fresh northwest wind with
a hint of chill in it. After he had breakfast and cleaned
up, he hobbled slowly out onto the beach, dragging an
ancient gray navy blanket.

After he had baked for nearly an hour, Betty Larkin
said, "Good morning! I guess you feel better." She
beamed down at him and dropped lithely into a Buddha
pose on the corner of his blanket. She wore a pale
gray one-piece swim suit with small blue flowers embroi-
dered on it. She carried a white rubber cap and a big
towel.

"I feel just fine. I feel just a little bit better than if
I was poking myself in the eye with a stick."

"I saw you out here, so I went in and changed. Hope you don't mind?"

"Not a bit. If I don't have to swim too."

"But you do! I heard Gil tell you to."

"I know. But I haven't got any character."

"Come on now! Come on!"

He groaned as he stood up. He followed her to the water. She tucked that bright heavy hair into the rubber cap and dived in and swam out. He paddled very slowly and tentatively, floating often, until, much sooner than he would have thought possible, some of the pain and stiffness began to leave his muscles. And he began to extend himself. He swam beside her, and they swam out to the unexposed sand bar a couple of hundred yards out. He swam with the untutored ease and confidence of any Floridian born and raised near the water. His stroke, he knew, looked clumsy, but it got him through the water quickly and without thrash or great effort. She was a superb swimmer. He knew she had had coaching. She was as sleek and swift and graceful as an otter.

They stood on the bar, facing each other. The water came to her shoulders.

"I talked to Donnie last night. First he tried to laugh it off. Then he got mad. He told me it wasn't any of my business. But I just got twice as mad as he did, and he finally got it through his thick head that I would make trouble for him, all that I possibly could, if he touches you again. And then he pretended that a great light had suddenly dawned on him and he . . ." she paused and looked toward the shore, her face coloring slightly under the deep tan ". . . said he didn't know we were in love. And even if I wasn't showing much taste, he wouldn't beat up any boy friend of mine. It was just his way of saving face. He knows better than that." She laughed in a bitter and humorless way. "I guess the whole town knows better than that. In his own way, he was being as nasty as he could."

"I don't know what you mean about the whole town."

"It's a long dull story. Anyway, he got the message."

"And thank you. It's a pleasure hiding behind your skirts. I would like to meet him some time outside the state of Florida."

"And I had a scrap with Buddy. No sister of his, by God, was going to be buddying around with no sneak thief. I told him you didn't do it, and why you'd said you had. So he said it looked like I'd swallow anything you felt like telling me. I . . . got him straightened out after a while. Now he'd like to see you. But he won't come out here. I would like to have you stop at the yard. Sort of casual-like. I mean, if you're going to settle here, Alex, it's people like Buddy who will make the difference."

"I'll stop by some time, Betty."

"Good."

They swam back in. She toweled herself, pulled off the cap, fluffed her hair, sat on the blanket and took one of his cigarettes. He stretched out near her. She sat looking out toward the water, hugging her knees. She had missed one portion of her back when she had dried herself. The sun-silver droplets of water stood out against the deep warm brown of her shoulder.

"About what I said last night, Alex."

"Yes?"

"About if you were playing a part or something. I guess you thought I was crazy. I guess that ever since . . . Jenna died, the whole town has been a little bit crazy. There were so many people prying. It's terrible the way they flock around. Oh, Donnie Capp had a ball. He really did. Some of them were crackpots and some were free-lance magazine writers and some were amateur detectives. Donnie ran them out just as fast as they came in. The business people weren't too happy about them being run off, but Donnie had the go-ahead from Sheriff Lawlor. There was some trouble about one man, about what they did to him over in Davis in the court house, but Donnie and two of the other deputies swore the man tried to run and fell down a flight of stairs, so nothing came of it. Donnie has said a hundred times that sooner or later, all by himself, he's going to get his hands on the man that killed Jenna. He takes it as a kind of personal insult that it should happen right in his own area. You know, after they locked up just about everybody who'd been in the Mack that night, Donnie, they say, got six or seven confessions before the sheriff pulled him off because there were too many newspaper people in town. Maybe he will find out someday. I hope he does, and on the other hand, I sort of hope he doesn't. Because then it will be the same thing all over again, and maybe worse with a trial and all. And it was very hard on Mother. You know, they'd come stand in the side yard and stare at the house with their mouths hanging open, like so many morons.

"Anyway, Alex, we've gotten so conditioned to people trying to pry that I got the crazy idea maybe somebody had sent you back here to . . . write it up or something. I guess you could find out . . . personal things that an outsider couldn't. For one of those terrible slander magazines. I guess it was a silly idea."

"You have my word of honor that I'm not here to write up the story of Jenna."

She turned and smiled at him. "I guess it's just an idea that somebody should have thought of. How about me helping you find something to do, Alex? What have you been thinking about doing?"

"Sounds like I'm becoming some sort of a project."

"Maybe. Anyway, to keep the record straight, you don't have to worry that maybe I'm moving in on you in any kind of . . . emotional way. I'd just like . . . to be your friend, Alex. I like to be with you because you don't . . . get sloppy ideas and try to put your hands on me. That is sort of . . . what Donnie was referring to."

"I don't know what you mean."

"This is a small town and it's all public knowledge, and somebody will tell you all about it sooner or later, and they may get it all twisted, so I'll tell you first. So you won't make any . . . mistakes. Now you roll over the other way. It's easier to talk to your back on this topic."

"If it's something that makes you that uncomfortable, I don't have to hear it."

"I think I'd like you to hear it from me so you'll hear it truthfully. I was eleven when you left. And I guess it was all starting at about that time. Or maybe earlier. Jenna was Daddy's favorite. He had no time for me or Buddy. As if he had only just enough love for one of his kids. When we were little, he used to call Sunday Jenna's day. And whenever it was nice weather, they'd go off together on a Sunday picnic, sometimes in the car but almost always in that old skiff of his. I guess Buddy used to think the same way I did that when we got to be older, we'd go too. But it never turned out that way. Even though Jenna was six years older, I tried to be exactly like her. So he'd love me too. And get things for me the way he did for her. Little surprises, special things when he went on trips. And swing me up in his arms and laugh and call me his girl. But no matter how hard I tried to be just like her, it never worked, Alex. And so I began to feel that there was something wrong with me. Something terrible that I didn't know about and nobody would tell me. I used to try to guess what it was.

"And finally, as I kept on growing and growing, I decided that it was because I was so big and ugly. Jenna was so dainty and pretty and little. That was a quality I couldn't duplicate. When I was about eight, Daddy began to have trouble with Jenna. Some kind of trouble I didn't understand. She lost interest in going on picnics

with him or anything like that. And he started beating
her for the first time, and then buying her presents to
make up. Usually he would beat her because she came
home so late. And when he'd tell her she couldn't go
out, she'd sneak out. I was secretly glad because I knew
he was going to stop loving her and begin loving me.
And I wouldn't be bad the way Jenna was being bad.
I couldn't understand why she wouldn't go on picnics.
You remember when Jenna ran away. Daddy was like a
crazy man. He spent a lot of money hiring people to find
her and bring her home, but nobody could find her.
And then he just seemed to pull way back inside of himself, where nobody could reach him.

"About a year later, after I was twelve, I was invited
to a party on Saturday afternoon. Daddy was home that
day. I had a blue dress, a new one for the party. He
was sitting in the living room, reading some kind of
business papers. I remembered how Jenna used to go to
him and turn around like a model when she was dressed
up for a party. And he would call her his girl friend
and tell her how pretty she was. I guess I had some
idea of cheering him up. And I did want him to be nice
to me. So I went in and held my arms out and started
turning around and around. It made me a little dizzy.
After a little while he yelled for my mother. 'Lila!' he
roared. 'Lila, come get revolving scarecrow out of here!' "

"What a filthy thing to do!"

"I ran upstairs and locked myself in my room. I
wouldn't come out. I didn't go to the party. I cut up
the blue dress until there wasn't one piece bigger than
a postage stamp. And I refused to wear another dress
until I went away to Gainesville after Daddy died. I
was a big scarecrow, and jeans and shorts and khakis
were good enough for scarecrows. That's part of it, part
of the reason, I guess.

"Anyway, by the time I was fourteen, I had a pretty
good knowledge of what Jenna's local career had been

like. I won't mince words, Alex. It was as if she had some strange kind of disease. Most of the boys she knew and a lot of men, married and single, in the county had lifted her little skirts, practically by invitation. I don't know when or how it started. Or why. I know she had matured early, and I know I certainly didn't. At fifteen I still looked like a skinny boy. Maybe I wanted to be a boy. I don't know. But in the six months before Daddy died, I suddenly turned into the same approximate shape I still am. Sort of bovine, I guess you could call it.

"And I certainly didn't want to follow in Jenna's footsteps. She'd been gone a long time but they still talked about her. Dirty talk. It offended me. My ideas of romance were highly platonic. I wanted no part of kissing games. I was going to prove that there could be a Miss Larkin who could stay off her back, excuse the expression.

"In my freshman year I came back for Christmas vacation. All my friends were back. There was a big holiday dance at the high school auditorium. I had a date. There was a lot of drinking going on, out in the automobiles. And a rough element was hanging around, quite a few of them from Davis. By the time I realized my date was coming apart at the seams, he was too drunk to drive me home. I didn't want to spoil anybody else's fun by asking for an early ride home. So I started to walk it. It's only about a mile.

"I got about a hundred yards from the auditorium. And suddenly, there in the dark, there were three men around me. They wanted to know where I was going all by myself. They smelled like 'shine. I tried to run and they grabbed me and took me around behind the gym. I kept trying to scream and fight, but they kept clamping their grimy hands over my mouth, and they kept hitting me so that I was dazed. They ripped most of my clothes off, and two of them held me down. I could hear the band playing in the auditorium. If they hadn't been quite so drunk, I wouldn't have had a chance in the world. But I kept kicking and bucking and squirming. I think one of them was trying to knock me out. Then somebody drove in and when they came to that turn in front of the gym, the headlights shone on the little scene and it scared them. Just then, thank God, the music stopped and I got my mouth free and yelled. And the car backed up so the lights were on us again. They took off. It was Ben Jeffry, coming to get his daughters. He had an old blanket in the car and he wrapped it around me. I was blubbering like a big baby. He took me to the doctor and even though I begged him not to make a fuss, he phoned the sheriff's office and reported it as rape. Sheriff Lawlor himself came over. By then word had gotten to the dance somehow. Buddy was there, stag, and he came to the doctor's office and then went home and got me some clothes. I wasn't marked up too badly. I did develop two dandy black eyes, and I was cut on the inside of the mouth. I didn't know who the men were, and I couldn't describe them, and I couldn't have identified them anyway.

"You know this town, Alex. There was more damn talk. I felt as if I couldn't walk down the street without people running out of their houses to stare at me. By the time the gossips got through with it, it was rape instead of attempted rape, and there had been a whole gang of them, and I was pregnant. And, as I learned later, there was one contingent that said that after all I was Jenna's sister and I had been drinking and carrying on, and when I was caught I'd started screaming to make people believe it was rape, and I certainly knew who the men were. Very pretty.

"Well, I didn't really stop being shaky until the following summer. I had a recurrent nightmare that lasted almost until then. But I had begun to wonder about myself. When a boy at school put his hand on my shoulder it made my stomach turn over. And the idea of ever kissing anyone terrified me. I told myself I'd have to stop being silly. After all, I certainly wanted a home and kids eventually. And I decided to cure myself. Poor Billy Hillyard. He'd always been kind of sappy about me. I guess some men like the big cowy type. So I encouraged him. I didn't see how Billy could upset me. So I gave him the right chance to kiss me that summer. And I stood it just as long as I could and then I had to push him away and jump out of the car and be terribly, horribly sick. I told Billy it was probably food poisoning. But, almost a month later, when exactly the same thing happened, he lost interest.

"In my junior year it seemed to be getting worse instead of better. I went to a woman doctor in Gainesville. I told her my sad story. She satisfied herself that I was normal physically in every respect and sent me to a psychiatrist in Tampa. I told him my problem. I told him about the attempted rape. He asked a lot of questions and he seemed much more interested in my childhood, in the father relationship and the sister relationship. I saw him three times. Then he summarized. My basic instincts were normal. But I could not react properly because of an extreme and artificial frigidity that was the direct result of the pattern of my home life. If I could spend eighteen months to two years in deep analysis, he might be able to help me. That was impossible, for many reasons. And then the damndest thing happened. When I came home for spring vacation, I found that it was all over town. Just about everybody knew the intriguing fact that I had gone to a psychiatrist because I was scared to death of men. I soon found out how *that* had happened. The Tampa doctor had asked the name of my family doctor. And, I suppose as a professional courtesy, he had sent old Dr. Bormen a detailed report. Maybe you remember that Heeley woman who worked for him. She talked all over town about every treatment Doc Bormen ever gave. And she had spread the news, but good. Talk about invasion of privacy.

"But here is the worst thing about it, Alex. In some crazy way it made me a project for every Don Juan who heard about it. As if I were his personal Sleeping Beauty. And he was just the one to do me the enormous personal favor of waking me up. I was inundated by spooks. And they were all so terribly hurt that I wouldn't even give them a chance. Nobody would have to know a thing about it. I should just co-operate and try not to be afraid.

"They've given up now, most of them. But I'm still one of the town's more notorious crazies. I don't date, and I don't expect to. They watch me. And I suppose it's common knowledge that this is the third time I've been out here. You can understand now how Donnie was being nasty. I like the work at the yard. I like swimming and sailing the *Lady Bird*. I am quite content, thank you, but I do sometimes miss the opportunity of having a normal and uncomplicated friendship with a man. Too much girl talk bores me rigid. So that's it. Don't try to make me your project, Alex. I've filed away those dreams of the joker on the white horse who was always killing a fat dragon who looked like Mr. Bolley. I am resigned to my busy spinsterhood. Even though I think you a very nice guy, Alex, and it's good to see you after all these years, if you were to lay a hand on me in anything but accident or physical assistance, it would chill me to the very marrow of my bones. And as far as being held and kissed by a man, I would much rather stick my head into a bucket of snakes."

"I keep seeing that kid in the blue dress, wanting to be admired."

"So do I, Alex. She was so vulnerable. She can break my heart. You won't mind being a friend of the curious and unnatural Miss Larkin?"

"Not at all. I'm honored, Miss Larkin."

She grinned at him. "Thanks. Say, is there any bread and anything to put between it?"

She made hefty sandwiches and they ate them on the beach. She went back to work. He baked himself in the sun and thought about her. It seemed curious that she should have such a distorted idea of her own appearance. That was probably part of the quirk. She thought of herself as big, bungling, bovine, cowy. At about five nine and an estimated hundred and thirty-five or forty pounds, she was certainly not tiny. But in the configuration of her body, in the walk and the grace of her, she was superbly feminine.

And, to his own wry amusement, he found himself composing mental charades in which he taught her that she could fulfill her role as a woman. It was a tantalizing situation, and he suspected that any other attitude toward her would be rather less than normal. But it was, of course, impossible. At the very first gesture toward any kind of intimacy, she would be off and running, never to look back.

He swam again, deliberately taxing the sore muscles, getting a certain satisfaction out of feeling the stretching and the pain. The club lumps on his skull were smaller, but still tender to the touch.

He showered and dressed and, at five o'clock, drove over into town. He went to Bolley's Hardware and bought another spinning rig and got a receipted bill to give Celia M'Gann. He had time to pick up some more groceries. He saw Junie Hillyard in the supermarket. As soon as she recognized him, she deliberately turned her back.

He started back toward the beach but, on impulse, just as he reached the foot of Bay Street he turned left on Front Street and drove along the bay shore and parked across from the Spanish Mackerel. As he walked toward the Mack he saw that it had changed very little. It was still a fisherman's bar that managed to look like a seedy lunchroom.

The late afternoon sunlight flooded in through the front windows. It sat in shabby patience looking across the street toward a fishing dock and boats and rotted pilings, and a pelican sitting on a slanting channel marker, and the green jungly growth of Ramona Key beyond the blue bay water.

The walls of the Mack were painted a soiled cream and green, cluttered with calendars, smutty mottoes, dusty mounted fish, pieces of net and old cork floats. There were warped venetian blinds at all the windows. The bar was on his left as he went in, topped with that imitation marble that used to be used on soda fountains. There were a dozen wooden bar stools stained dark. On his right were a dozen round tables with green formica tops in a green that clashed with the green on the walls. Across the back wall was a huge juke box, and two pin-ball machines, and a bowling game machine, a wall phone, an open door that exposed a narrow dingy area containing a blackened hamburg grill and a big tarnished coffee urn; a closed door that, he remembered, gave access to a back room for card games, a kitchen, a staircase to the upstairs where Harry Bann lived.

The only customer was a man sitting on the stool farthest from the entrance. He wore a blue work shirt and denim pants, with the shirt sleeves rolled high to expose muscular arms thickly matted with curly black hair. He had an empty beer bottle and an empty glass in front of him. In profile his face looked dark and predatory under a forehead so high and bulging that it gave him something of the look of a surly embryo. The girl behind the bar was leaning on it and talking to the man in a voice so low that Doyle could not distinguish a word. But it all had the flavor of argument. She gave Doyle a casual glance when he took the stool nearest the door and returned to the inaudible wrangle.

He sat and stared at a card of potato chips, a jar of evil-looking pickles, a peanut machine, dusty liquor bot-

tles aligned in front of a long blue panel of mirror, a
chrome paper-napkin dispenser, a withered menu with a
water-skiing maiden on the front, a squeeze bottle of
catsup and one of mustard, both obviously used often and
carelessly, two busy flies on the coffee-spattered rim of a
thick china sugar bowl, one poster announcing a dance
over in Wellsland that had taken place two months ago,
an ancient cash register which sat on a smeared glass
case containing cigarettes, cigars, candy and, incongru-
ously, a small plastic Santa Claus with a face of discontent.

He waited patiently, becoming more and more aware
of the effluvia of stale grease, spilled beer and elderly
nicotine. More subtle were the drifting odors of rancid
coffee, perfume, fish scales, armpits, bad plumbing, and
the nausea of ten thousand Saturday nights.

The girl finally walked down toward Doyle, a girl in
her early twenties he guessed, with carroty red hair, a
moon face lightly pocked with old acne scars, small features squeezed together in the middle of an expression
of surly petulance, a pinched discontent. She had made
her mouth vast and square with a shade of lipstick that
did not suit her. She wore tight threadbare red shorts, a
faded red halter, a small stained apron. Her figure was
heavy, but reasonably good. Her skin had that damp and
luminous blue-whiteness of cheap lard and overturned fish.
When she walked she set her heels down so heavily she
awakened little jinglings among the racked glasses, and
her large breasts and heavy thighs joggled most unpleas-
antly.

He ordered a beer and watched her walk back to the
beer cooler, the pulpy buttocks working under the frayed
red fabric. From her coloring he guessed she was some
kin to Harry Bann's wife. Mrs. Bann had been a meaty
carroty woman who had often come to visit Doyle's
mother at the hotel, and who had died that same winter
Mary Ann Doyle had died. Some kind of kidney trouble.

She banged the beer down in front of him, slapped his change from fifty cents on the bar top and went back to her friend. The old man he had seen reading the comic book in Ducklin's shuffled in, talking gently to himself. He threw down a double shot and trudged out. The hairy embryo stood up and snarled something at the girl.

"So *never* come back!" she yelled. "So who *cares?*"

The man left. The screen-door cylinder hissed wearily as the door swung shut. The girl sighed and began to mop the counter listlessly, working her way down toward Doyle.

"Not much business," he said.

"Friday and Saddy there's more."

"You related to Harry?"

She stopped mopping and stared at him, her eyes small and pale and blue and suspicious. "I'm his niece. Who's asking?"

"My name is Doyle. I used to live here."

Her face brightened. "Hey, you're the one! I hear people talking about you. My brothers were in, talking about you. Lee and Gil. I'm Janie Kemmer. My ma was Miz Bann's sister. Gil says you and him used to fight. How long you been gone?"

"Fifteen years."

"Then I wouldn't remember on account of I was three or four years old."

"I met Lee when I first got back."

"And he was drunk, I bet." She sighed. "They just don't seem to give a damn. They do a little fishing and they hire out on construction sometimes, but most of the work they do is free road work when Donnie Capp picks them up for drunk or fighting. Gil was sent away once for four years. It was just a fight right out behind here in the lot, with a drunk tourist. He was sort of old but he wanted real bad to fight Gil, so that's how come it was only manslaughter. Now Lee is back on road work. Donnie picked him up last night again." She smirked. "Old

Lee, he sure is funny sometimes. He didn't have a ride back down to Bucket Bay and he was trying to steal a boat."

"It looked to me like you were having a fuss with your friend sitting up the other end of the bar."

She looked desolate. "That Charlie is a jerk. I been going with him three years; and now I want to get married, he wants to go back in the navy. All the time he says when I'm eighteen we get married and everything is fine. Now he wants to go in the navy." The blue eyes suddenly began to leak tears. "God *damn* him!" she said, and snatched a paper napkin, turned her back and blew her nose.

Doyle sat uncomfortably until she turned back and said, "I din't mean to pop off. Only he gets me so mad. Only he's twenty-eight, and how long should you wait anyhow? I'm supposed to hang around here and wait or something. Nothing ever happens here. Nothing!"

"From what I've heard since I've been back, a lot has been happening around here, Janie."

"Oh, you mean the murder. Well, that was something, I guess. But how many of those do you get? I mean how often? Every hundred years or something. Oh, I don't mean there hasn't been killings. Knifings and like that. The last time there was a murder-type murder, it was a long time ago, down in Bucket Bay. I guess I was maybe nine or ten. When that old Paul Garnette, him that had all the kids, got caught by that Casey Myers when Paul was fooling around with Casey's fifteen-year-old daughter, the one that wasn't right in the head. Casey grabbed a gaff and yanked him off. Got him right in the throat with the gaff, and then that girl really went nuts. They had to put her away some place. Casey was only in jail overnight and it didn't get into all the big papers like when Jenna was murdered. God, this little ole town sure was jumping. Harry and I liked to work ourselves to death. Those newspaper people drink almost as fast as the commercial fishermen."

"I used to know a lot of the commercial fishermen."

"I guess there was a lot more fifteen years ago, Mr. Doyle. Plenty of them moved further south, and a lot of them got out of the business, they say. There's empty shacks down to Bucket Bay, just standing there rotting. They can still make it on the shrimps, but they got to go to Tampa or Key West to ship out."

She excused herself to go greet two young men in sweaty khakis and serve them beer at the far end of the bar. She talked with them for a little while and then she came back to him. There was just enough coquetry in her walk and manner so that he suspected that he had been considered as a possible substitute for the uncooperative Charlie.

"That's a real pretty sport shirt, Mr. Doyle."

"Thanks."

"What's your line of work?"

"Nothing right now. I'm looking around. Maybe I might pick up a used dozer and see if I can get some land-clearing work."

"There isn't as much of that to do around here as there is other places. But there's some. Don't they cost a lot?"

"I've got a little ahead. I just came back from working in Venezuela."

"God, I'd like to travel some. I'd like to see me some far away places. Nothing *ever* happens here."

"Except a murder every once in a while."

"Now you just stop teasing me, Mr. Doyle."

"Alex."

"That's a nice name. I like that name."

"I heard Jenna was in here the night she got killed."

She glanced toward the two boys and lowered her voice. "I've got orders from Harry not to talk about it to strangers. I don't see what difference it makes. It gets talked about a lot in here. And sometimes you wonder if maybe somebody talking or listening is the one did it." She hugged herself with her heavy white arms and gave a little shiver. "That's kind of creepy. Anyhow, I guess it's because Donnie Capp doesn't want any strangers around prying. He runs 'em off. I guess he's maybe afraid somebody might by accident pry around and find out who did it before Donnie finds out. He's got to be the one who gets the killer because it's a matter of pride. The big shots sorta pushed him out of the way last fall when they were investigating. But since you come from here, I guess you aren't a stranger. She was in here all right that night. Friday night. I went off at six on account of Harry doesn't like me working at night, especially on a Friday or Saddy night when things can get rough around here real fast and a girl can't walk across the room without wise guys grabbing at her. But she was here before I went off and she stayed until closing. And then she walked right out and got herself strangled. I couldn't hardly believe it when I heard it the next morning. I wanted to get to see her at Jeffry Brothers, but that sister of Colonel M'Gann had fixed it so nobody could get to see her but the family, and they say the colonel didn't get to see her even. On account of his bad heart."

"I guess Jenna wasn't much like her kid sister."

"I swear I don't see how those two came out of the same family. You know, Betty comes in here a lot."

"She does!"

"The boat yard is just down the road another two blocks, you know. And all the fishermen, they think she's the finest damn thing on legs. When old Spence Larkin was alive they say he wouldn't touch a commercial boat unless it was cash on the line. But she works things out with them so they can get work done when they have to have it. And she'll stop in here and have a beer with them. Usually in the afternoon, but sometimes in the

evening. And you don't see anybody making any grabs
at her. If anybody did, all her boatyard customers would
tear the poor guy's head off and use the rest of him for
chum. Not that anybody but some stranger would get
fresh with her, him not knowing about her. There's
something wrong with her. She looks like a lot of woman
but she isn't. Something terrible happened to her a long
time ago, and she just isn't any good for anything. God,
I'd hate to be like that. I guess it just about wouldn't
be worth living, wouldn't you say?"

"I guess so."

"That Jenna was just the other way around. She
couldn't get enough. Funny, isn't it? Right out of the
same family. I don't know if Donnie will ever find who
killed her. Some nights people come from a long way
off and drive out to the beach. Me, I think it was somebody like that, from the other end of the county. It
would be easier if she was raped, because then it could
maybe have been a Negro. But she wasn't, and I guess
that just about every Negro for fifty miles around must
know that Donnie checks that beach every now and then
and if he caught any of them out there, he'd play hell with
them for sure. I think it was some stranger and she
got in some kind of drunk argument and got choked.
And they took off. Or maybe somebody beached a boat.
But one thing, I don't think that Donnie will give up
looking."

"I guess everybody has their own ideas."

"Some of them are pretty crazy. Some people say it
was on account of the money. They say she got killed
because she knew where Spence Larkin hid all the money
they never found. So they caught her there on the beach
and they killed her and then they went and dug it up.
They made her tell where it was. That's plain silly, because the night she was killed she came in here without
a dime. Harry'd said not to let her have any more on
credit. But there was always somebody to buy her a drink.

If she was out of money and knew where it was, she would have gone and dug it up, wouldn't she?"

"Looks like she would."

"Nobody is ever going to find that money except by some kind of accident maybe. And then I bet there won't be much left of it. Not in this climate."

She looked toward the doorway and her face changed in an almost dramatic way, becoming instantaneously blank, almost sleepy. Doyle heard the screen-door cylinder hiss.

He turned and saw Deputy Donnie Capp standing just inside the door. "Hello, Doyle," he said. "Hello, Janie."

"Hello, Mr. Capp," she said faintly.

Capp moved in on Doyle's left and stood at the bar. Doyle could scent the animal sharpness of Capp's perspiration.

"Hear Charlie's going in the navy, Janie."

"I guess that's right."

"Maybe you took off twenty pounds and stopped stuffing that hungry gut of yours, you'd look better than the navy. Harry should have pounded your butt for you the very first time you started sneaking off in the brush with that Charlie. You was so sure of Charlie, Janie, you let yourself get real sloppy. Now what you going to do? Want I should pick you a husband off the road gang? Anything I tell those boys to do, they'll do, no matter how it could ugly up their future."

Tears had started to roll down her white face, but she couldn't seem to look away from Donnie.

"You trot all that beef up the other end of the bar, Janie. I got words with Mr. Doyle here. I got to call him mister now."

She moved away, slowly and heavily. Capp said, "If the slut had a head on her, she'd grab Harry. They aren't blood kin. He's got the asthma and the high-blood pressure, and she'd end up with a good little business instead of it going to his brother."

Doyle lifted his beer glass and drank, and was remotely pleased to see that he could keep his hand from trembling.

"You don't have much to say for yourself, Mr. Doyle."

"I guess not."

"Heard you just as I got near the door. You and Janie talking about Jenna. Guess you knew Jenna before she took off with that sailor boy. That was when you were a big athlete. Before you took up stealing. Knew her, didn't you?"

"Yes."

"Now you're getting to know the sister awful damn fast. Can't see why the Larkins should give a damn what happens to you. Seems real strange to me. And there you are, right out there on the beach near to where she was killed, and near the colonel and his sister. And I've got the word to keep my hands off you. Funny."

"Is there something you want?"

"It don't make much sense, but I find myself wondering if somehow somebody brought you back here to look into the Jenna killing. You got you a oily satisfied look, like an egg-sucking hound dog. I'd hate to find out you were sticking your nose in something that's none of your business. I just might have to naturally take this here club and loosen up your insides a little."

"Why?"

"Because you'd be getting in the way of the law. We can handle everything that has to be done our own selves."

Capp moved away, silent in the black boots. The screendoor hissed behind him.

A few minutes later, as Doyle got up to leave, an old man came in, a brown old man with soiled white hair, bleached eyes and a white stubble of beard. He stared at Doyle for a moment and said, "Say, I bet you're Bert Doyle's boy. You look a lot like Bert when he was alive, afore he got drownded that time."

"That's right. I'm Alex Doyle."

"And you don't know me at all?"

"Wait a minute. Arnie Blassit?"

"Dead right, boy. When I was fishing shares with old Lucas Pennyweather, you come along with us a lot of times. You made a good hand, for a kid."

Doyle sat at the bar again and bought a beer for himself and a drink for Blassit. Blassit talked about old times, about the half-remembered people Alex had known before his father died.

"It's not like it used to be, boy. It's getting all fished out. We got no closed season on mullets now, but snook is a game fish and you can't make a catch on trouts any more. I kinda hang on. Too damn old to learn new tricks."

"How about Lucas Pennyweather? Is he still around?"

"No. He was getting pretty crippled up. And last November a grown daughter of his come all the way down from North Carolina and she and her husband, they took Lucas back up to live with them. One day you'd think he was going to be here forever, and the next day he was gone. It was real sudden. Sold his boat and gear, but sold 'em so fast it was damn near giving them away. I tell you, there was nobody knew these waters any better than Lucas. Some will tell you Spence Larkin knew more, but I say Lucas Pennyweather."

"He liked kids. I can remember going out with him when I couldn't have been more than three or four years old."

And suddenly Doyle remembered a scene that had been buried for years. Old Lucas had taken a half dozen kids out with him on a Sunday to fish with hand lines in a grouper hole not far outside Windy Pass. And on the way back they had passed a small white skiff with a man at the wheel and a little girl sitting in the bow. The little girl was blond and she wore a pink dress, and to Alex, about six at the time, she was the cleanest prettiest thing he had ever seen.

"There goes Spence Larkin and his daughter," Lucas had told them. "He's a big important man there in Ramona, and that's his eldest. He takes her on picnics of a Sunday, down there in those bay islands some place."

Alex remembered that he had turned and watched the small girl until she was lost in the sunny distances of the bay. And later he had seen Spence Larkin many times alone in the same skiff. It was his commonly known eccentricity to leave his office at the boat yard at any time of day and go off down the bay alone. People said that was where he did his thinking. People said he would go out in that skiff with its ancient engine and chug along and plot new meanness, new ways to make a dollar grow from a dime. He always took a fishing rod and a tackle box that he kept in his office, but he didn't do much fishing.

Arnie Blassit chuckled and said, "Just about the last thing old Lucas did in this town was get himself arrested on suspicion of murder. Didn't mean anything. Everybody who'd been right here in the Mack the night Jenna Larkin got choked to death, they got picked up. Me too. But me and Lucas, we could clear each other. We run out of drinking money along about eleven, and we were sharing a shack down to Chaney's Bayou, and we had come up in my boat and tied her right across the road there. So about eleven we went on back down the bay together and the first thing we knew about it, them deputies come and took us all the way over to Davis and locked us up. Let us go the next day. Lucas sure was mad. Thing was, he'd spent some time talking to Jenna that night. I thought about that. It was as if the Lord give her one final chance to be nice to somebody and she took it."

"How do you mean?"

"Up to that last night she didn't have any time or any politeness to spare for any old beat-down fishermen.

There was a good crowd and after we'd been in a few minutes, standing right over there, she come over to us and was real nice. She wanted to talk about the old days. And after a while she took Lucas right over there to that corner table, and they sat there and talked a long time. And when it finally broke up, some of us were kidding Lucas till he got pretty mad about the whole thing. And then he made it worse for himself by saying that he'd made a date with her to go out in the boat the next day and look around the bay islands. Matter of fact, Alex, when they come and took us to Davis, Lucas was just getting ready to take the boat on up to the yard and pick Jenna up. But she was dead by then. And it sure upset Lucas to hear about it."

"I guess the whole town was upset from what I hear."

Blassit chuckled again. "I see that Donnie Capp leaving as I come down the street a little while ago. Now I guess he was the one most upset. That boy is just as mean as a snake. And he'd been trying to move in on Jenna. Now there's a lot of things people called her, but nobody called her especially choosey when it come to men. But she wouldn't have a thing to do with that Donnie Capp. She just laughed at him. I've heard that Donnie has made some gals real willing by roughing 'em up a little first, but he couldn't take a club to Jenna and get away with it. Matter of fact, he was the one broke up Jenna's nice little talk with Lucas. Went right over and sat with them without any invitation, and after a while she got tired of him listening, so she went away. Donnie sat there and talked to Lucas for a while, and then he left. I guess Donnie thought he was getting close to talking Jenna into something, because he sure acted like a crazy man after he found she'd been killed. He put knots on half the heads in the county until the sheriff got him soothed down some."

"Arnie, I've got to run along. It's been good to see you again."

He drove back out to the cottage. After he had un-loaded his purchases he took a walk on the beach until the afterglow of the sunset had died to streaks of yellow and green close to the western horizon.

He fixed a simple supper, and after he had cleaned up he sat and smoked in the dark on the little screened porch and thought about the days of childhood. The vivid memory of Jenna in the pink dress had aroused other memories. They were memories of the other life that he had tried to forget, telling himself that it had all been bad. But in the reawakened memories there was much that was good.

And later he began to think about Jenna. And he began to wonder why she had been pleasant to old Lucas. She must have had some reason. There must have been some-thing she wanted.

chapter SEVEN

ON FRIDAY MORNING at eleven, Alex walked up the beach to the Proctor cottage, carrying the two spinning rods. When he was a hundred feet from the porch, Celia M'Gann came out and walked to meet him.

"I expected you yesterday, Mr. Doyle."

"Sure sorry about that, but something came up."

"You didn't have those terrible bruises on your arms and legs. Did you fall?"

"Guess you could say I fell into a deputy sheriff, ma'am. He came out to have a little talk with me. He talked with a club, mostly. That was Wednesday, and I was too stiffened up to get much done yesterday."

"Were you drinking? Why did he hit you?"

"Sort of on general principles, I guess."

"Was it a man named Capp?"

"That's him. Donnie Capp."

"I had difficulty with that man. I don't like him at all. He was determined to bother the colonel. And I was just as determined that he wouldn't. He was very rude."

"Here's the stuff I bought for your brother."

"How much do I owe you?"

"Here's the receipt, ma'am."

She told him to wait and went into the house and came out with the exact amount in cash, and said that the colonel would be out in a few moments.

Colonel M'Gann came out of the cottage and came slowly down the steps. He was a big man, almost uncomfortably thin, but with the look and bearing of someone who had once been much heavier. He had gray hair like his sister, and the same strong planes and structure of face. He wore rope sandals, khaki shorts. He was tanned, but it was tan over an unhealthy skin tone. There was a strange remoteness about him, not coolness or unfriendliness, but merely a vast indifference.

"The mackerel was excellent, Mr. Doyle. My sister and I thank you." As he spoke Alex had the feeling that the colonel was looking through him and beyond him.

The three of them went to the water's edge, and Doyle showed Colonel M'Gann how to handle the spinning tackle. He learned with that special quickness possible only to people who combine manual dexterity with that sort of analytical mind which quickly perceives the purpose of each movement. Yet it seemed a sterile effort. M'Gann obviously had no interest in it, was merely attempting to please his sister.

"No point at all, Colonel, in standing out here and whipping up the water when you don't see any activity. Say, it looks like something going on up the beach there a ways."

Celia tagged along. But when they moved farther, she

said she would get lunch started and went back toward the house.

They caught several small jacks and released them. M'Gann said, "Thank you very much for the lesson, Mr. Doyle." He walked up onto the dry sand and sat down. "I think I'll rest for a few moments and then walk back to the house. I still tire easily."

Doyle sat beside him. "You better rinse the rod and reel off in fresh water when you get back."

"Yes, of course."

Doyle turned so he could watch M'Gann's face and said, "They are still having a great deal of trouble with the Henderson circuits, sir. They haven't gotten the bugs out yet."

For long moments the colonel still stared out toward the Gulf, his face impassive. And then he turned and looked at Doyle. The remoteness was gone. And Doyle was aware of the unforgettable impact of a truly strong personality.

"You're clever, Mr. Doyle. If that's your name. Who sent you?"

"Colonel Presser."

"I should have guessed. Austin has always had a taste for intrigue and melodrama."

"The problem was to contact you, sir. The strangers they sent down couldn't make it. Your sister has . . ."

"Celia has been very diligent about shielding me from all pleas and requests. This little subterfuge will annoy her. She can't seem to understand that I am willing to say no—to Austin Presser or anyone else."

"Can you tell me why you'd say no, Colonel? Is it . . . health?"

The colonel looked out across the Gulf. "I am getting stronger. As a civilian consultant, I could pace myself. But it is as if all that work was done by somebody else. Far away and long ago. I can't go back now, Doyle. I never thought that anything could become more im-

portant to me than my sense of duty and obligation.
Right now I have a personal problem. Call it an emotional problem. I don't intend to explain it to you. Until
it is solved, if it ever can be solved, I am . . . incapable of considering anything else."

"And if you solve this . . . emotional problem?"

"I can go back to work. And make Austin happy. But
you see, Mr. Doyle, one possible solution to my problem would be for me to see how far and fast I can run
down this beach."

"I don't understand."

"I don't expect you to understand. Sometimes a man
can find himself in a maze that seems insoluble. Labo-
ratory rats, faced with an insoluble maze, have been
known to give up and lie on their backs and nibble their
forepaws. I find that quite touching to contemplate. A
man in the process of trying to find a solution to what
seems to be an insoluble problem, Mr. Doyle, is not in-
clined to devote his time and energies to his profes-
sion, no matter how vital his work may be. I am sorry.
You may tell Austin I am sorry."

Doyle remembered with distaste the next phase of his
instructions. "Colonel Presser seems to feel that you
are brooding over the death of your wife, Colonel. He
has acquired a long and accurate file on her. It isn't
pleasant reading. I can give you some of the facts."

"I'm not interested, Doyle. I made a very bad marriage. It took me a long time to become aware of
how bad it was. My wife was a reckless, selfish, faith-
less woman. I met her at a time when she had a yearn-
ing for respectability, apparently."

"Then I don't understand."

"There is nothing for you to understand."

"Colonel M'Gann, if your wife's murderer was caught,
would you then be willing to go back to work?"

M'Gann looked at him quickly, with an odd expression,

as though Doyle had shocked him. Yet, to Doyle, it had seemed a most obvious question.

"I might."

"Here comes your sister. Are you going to tell her about this?"

"I see no point in telling her. I can't see that you have changed anything."

After Celia joined them and they walked back down the beach, M'Gann was again back in his shell. Celia was most friendly. Doyle refused her invitation to lunch. When he glanced back, they were going into the house. She was holding the screen door for the colonel.

Doyle walked slowly back toward his cottage. I might have something to tell you one of these days, Colonel, he thought. I might have a message for you. I'm beginning to see a pattern in things. I might even know why she was killed.

At two o'clock he drove by the Mack and turned in at the Larkin Boat Yard and Marina at the end of Front Street. He had remembered it as a place of clutter and corrosion, with sun-drab, sagging structures and docks, a general air of aimlessness.

But now white posts marked the entrance to a graveled parking area beside a small white office building. There were half a dozen cars in the lot in addition to the familiar jeep and a freshly painted pickup with the Larkin name on the door. When he got out of the car he could hear the busy chatter of office equipment and, farther away, the high whine of a wood saw and the roar of a motor under test. As he walked toward the office he could see three wide solid docks built out into the bay, with a T and bright gas pumps at the outer end of the nearest one. He could see a big covered work shed with the open side facing the bay, heavy ways and cradles, some warehouse structures, a covered boat-storage area with an aluminum roof that was blinding in the sunlight.

When he went into the office Betty was typing and a woman in her middle years was operating an adding machine. The interior was clean and bright and efficient looking.

Betty smiled with obvious pleasure, got up quickly and introduced him to the other woman, a Mrs. West, and then took him on a guided tour. Today she wore a dark red blouse and a red-and-white-striped skirt. The unruly hair, in all its streaks and shades of umber, toffee and cream, had been pulled back into a rebellious pony tail.

"This is certainly a different place from the one I remember."

"It's been a lot of work, Alex, building it up. And the bank still owns a pretty good hunk of it. But we're doing a good business. Got a total of fifteen on the payroll. We do good work and we get a lot of word-of-mouth advertising among boat people. That's the best kind. We can yank stuff out of the water up to seventy feet long. There's Buddy. I guess he's a lot bigger than when you left."

They walked toward a man who had his back turned to them while he scraped at the hull of a small twin-screw cruiser. He was a huge brown man with corn yellow hair worn a quarter of an inch long. He was well over six feet tall. He wore greasy shorts and sneakers. There was hair on his back and shoulders, bleached silvery white by the sun. His calves were like oaken kegs. He was wide and solid from top to bottom, like a tree.

When Betty spoke he turned. He had a brute jaw and small, gray, smoldering eyes under a solid ridge of brow. He could have played a villain part in a Viking movie.

"Glad to see you again, Alex," he said as they shook hands. Just as Alex was considering falling to his knees and howling like a dog, Buddy released his grip. "Hear Donnie welcomed you home."

"In a big way."

"We'll keep him off your back. He goes too damn far lately."

Alex suddenly realized that this prehistoric mammoth was ill at ease, actually quite shy. It amused him.

"I just remembered a phone call I should make," Betty said. "Why don't you show Alex around, Buddy, and introduce him to John Geer. When you've had the rest of the tour, Alex, you come back to the office and you can take me down the road and buy me a beer."

When Betty was out of sight, Buddy said, "This place wouldn't run right without her. I can't handle that office stuff. It drives me nuts. Come meet our partner, John Geer."

John Geer was working on a marine engine. He was grime to the elbows, a shambling man with a remote resemblance to Gary Cooper, but with brown eyes too close together and a pendulous lower lip.

Buddy showed him around the shop area. Alex could sense the man's devotion to good materials and fine workmanship. He showed him the warehouse. As they turned away from the warehouse Alex saw a trim little Thistle on a yellow trailer under a shed roof. The mast was stepped and lashed. He could see the name. The *Lady Bird*.

"Betty's?" he said.

"Her pet. She can really make it get up there and fly. And she'll take it out in the worst weather you ever saw."

"She's quite a gal, Buddy."

Buddy propped one foot on the trailer tire, lit a cigarette and shook the match. "She likes you, Alex."

"I'm glad of that."

"I . . . I don't want you should upset her."

"I know the score, Buddy. I got it from her. I've got no intention of upsetting her."

"I had to say it."

"I know."

"Well, I guess there isn't much else around here to see."

"That skiff there, Buddy. Wasn't that your father's?" He gestured toward a small skiff, pointed at both ends, with a center engine hatch and a horizontal wheel. The paint was fresh and it was up on stubby saw horses.

"That was his. We talk about putting a new engine in it and unloading it. But we never seem to get around to it."

"I want to ask you something, Buddy. You're a little older than Betty, so you might be able to remember more clearly than she could. I haven't asked her. I don't even want you to try to ask me why I'm asking such a question. When you were little, your father used to take Jenna on picnics all alone, didn't he?"

"In that same skiff. All the time."

"And Sunday was Jenna's day, wasn't it?"

"He spoiled her rotten, Alex. The way she turned out, it was his fault."

"Did he take her to a special place?"

"On the picnics? I don't think so."

"Can you remember anything about there being a special place?"

Buddy glared back into the past, motionless for long seconds. "There was a place. It's been a long time. Twenty years. Sure, she used to tease us about it. It was a big secret, she said. She wasn't supposed to tell."

"Can you remember anything she said about it?"

"No. All I can remember is that she used to make up all kinds of stuff. Why are you . . ." Buddy stopped suddenly and looked beyond Alex with an expression of surprise, almost of consternation, and said, as though speaking to himself, "That's where he could have hid the money."

"That's what I've been thinking."

Buddy looked directly at him, his face changing, growing hard and skeptical. "That's what you've been thinking, is it? Just who the hell are you, Doyle? What's this big fat interest in where the money is? What are all these questions?"

"Now wait a minute."

"Wait for what? I don't know where you came from. You show up here and sweet-talk Betty. Tell her you never stole a dime. She believes you. You get her to tell me you're such a nice guy."

"I didn't get her to tell you a thing, Larkin."

"What do I know about you? Maybe you've been in the can for years. You were one of Jenna's boy friends. You'd hear about the murder. The newspapers brought up how the old man's money was never found when they covered the murder. Tried to tie it in somehow, but it wouldn't hold together. How do I know how much Jenna told you and how much you remember? Now you come down here sucking around, asking questions. The hell with you, Doyle."

"Use your head, Buddy. If that was what I was after, why would I give it away talking to you this way?"

"I think you're a clever guy, Doyle. I think you're down here on the make for something. Maybe Donnie does too and that's why he whipped your skull for you."

"Do you want to find out who killed Jenna?"

"Sure, but . . ."

"Then we should put our heads together and try to figure out if it was tied in with the money your father hid."

"But why should you give a damn who killed Jenna?"

Doyle was momentarily trapped. He could not give his actual reason. And he couldn't think of any other convincing reason.

"You're just meddling," Buddy said. "So get off the place. Keep away from Betty. We can handle our own problems." And he pushed Doyle roughly.

And that push ignited a white flare in the back of the skull of Alex Doyle. He had been physically humiliated by Donnie Capp. He had been conscious of the public disapproval of his return. The emotional tensions and frustrations exploded into a hard overhand right that smacked the shelf of Buddy Larkin's jaw, knocked his mouth open, glazed his eyes, caused him to take two steps back and sit down heavily.

There was no one to see them in that sheltered area near the warehouse. The noise of the marine engine being test-run by Geer obscured any sounds of combat. After a moment of inert surprise, Buddy bounded up with disconcerting agility and lunged toward Doyle, chin on his chest, big fists held low. Doyle ducked and slipped two powerful hooks, looking for a chance to land solidly. Before he had his chance, a solid smash on the chest knocked him backward into the skiff. As Buddy reached for him, he scrambled out the far side and came around the stern. They met there. Doyle got in one solid blow and, without transition, found himself on hands and knees, shaking his head. He got up and, after a moment of blackout, found himself on his back. He wobbled to his feet and swung blindly at the vague shape moving toward him. His fist blazed with pain and with the effort of the blow, he knocked himself sprawling. He got up onto one knee. Buddy Larkin was sitting eight feet away. They stared at each other, sobbing for air. As Buddy got up, Doyle got up and raised his fists.

Buddy stared at him. "Knock it off. Can I whip you?"

"Yes, I guess you can," Doyle said in a remote, rusty voice.

"But you'll keep trying?"

"As long as I can keep getting up."

"Stubborn bastard," Buddy said glumly. He walked over to a hose faucet, bent over, caught water in his cupped hands and sloshed his face thoroughly. When he was through, Doyle knelt by the faucet and stuck his head under the stream.

"Am I marked?" Buddy asked.

"Just a lump on your jaw." Buddy touched the place and winced.

Doyle worked the fingers of his right hand. The knuckles were puffy. Buddy said, "You look okay."

"My mouth is cut on the inside."

They sat on a saw horse, still breathing more deeply than normal.

"Damn fool," Buddy said.

"I don't like to be pushed."

"All right. You don't like to be pushed. I'll make a note of it. To get back to the old man. He was always going off by himself. He'd come back from a business trip and almost the first thing, he'd be off in the skiff. He was such a secretive kind of guy. He must have had some place he'd go. Hell, he'd never go there direct. But he'd always head south down the bay, not that that will do us much good. Give me one of those cigarettes."

Doyle lit it for him. He felt sourly amused. The suspicion was gone. Buddy Larkin had made up his mind about him in his own special way. Possibly it was a better way than logic. In Larkin's book a man who kept getting up could be trusted.

"Here's something that might fit, Buddy," he said. "See what you think. The night Jenna was killed, she spent some time talking to old Lucas Pennyweather, and they were going to go out the next day in his boat. That's one of the things that started me thinking. She wouldn't have been nice to him unless she wanted something. You know that as well or better than I do. So maybe she wanted his help in finding the place where her father used to take her. Maybe she could remember enough so there was a good chance of Lucas finding the place she described."

Buddy nodded. "She wouldn't have been able to find it herself. She never had much interest in the water. And you know as well as I do what it's like down there in all those mangrove islands. God, there must be twenty thousand little islands. If she could remember a little, and anybody could help her, it would be old Lucas."

"And Lucas left shortly after she was killed."

He shook his head slowly. "Not Lucas, if that's what you're thinking. Not that old man. He didn't know his daughter was finally coming after him. She'd been threatening to for a long time. He came around to say good-by. A decent old guy, Alex."

"So then he didn't know what she was driving at—I mean if we've been making good guesses."

"Lucas was smart as hell about water and weather and fish and children. But he wasn't too bright about people. People like Jenna. He'd take everybody at face value. And you know how he liked to talk. She would never have said anything about money."

"You're right. Just ask him to take her to the places where her father used to take her. For old times' sake."

Buddy kicked the trailer tire. "All this is fine, Alex, but it leaves something up in the air. How come Jenna gets that idea all of a sudden?"

"I don't know. As you said, it was a long time ago. Twenty years. Maybe something reminded her. And she started thinking."

"But even if she was right, the money is still there. And she is dead, so even if Lucas wasn't gone, it wouldn't be possible to find it."

"Unless, Buddy, she described the place where she wanted to be taken especially. All she could remember of it. And Lucas said he thought he could find it, and promised to take her there."

"Then we ought to check with Lucas."

"It would be the only way. You've got the shore line of the keys and the shore line of the mainland, and then all those islands, Buddy. It would take years and years to cover the area, even if you had some idea of what you were looking for. You couldn't even look for a place that was kept cleared of brush because it's been nine years since your father made his last trip."

Buddy suddenly grinned in a mirthless way. "If you want any more proof, I've thought of something else. He kept that rod and the tackle box in his office. I went through that stuff after he died. A fair-sized tackle box, with just a couple of lures in it. Damn near empty. I looked around but I couldn't find the rest of the stuff I thought he must have carried in it. And I didn't think anything much about it until now. He liked cash deals. So he'd come back from selling off land with the cash, and he'd transfer it from his brief case to that tackle box, and tell somebody to get the skiff ready. And then he'd take off. Hell, when the big treasure hunt was on after he died, I thought he could have hidden the stuff somewhere down the bay. I guess everybody thought of that. But we just never thought of there being some specific place that he went to that somebody else might know about. We didn't remember about Jenna when she was little and was willing to go on picnics with him."

"Betty told me about Sunday being Jenna's day. I didn't think about there being a special place until Arnie Blassit told me about Jenna being nice to Lucas the night she was killed."

Buddy stared curiously at Alex. "It's the sort of thing the family should have figured out. Not an outsider. Funny you should have come up with a thing like this."

"I've had some practice adding bits and pieces of information together, trying to come up with some kind of pattern. I can tell you about it some time. But right now, we ought to get hold of Lucas. Do you know his address?"

"It's probably at the post office. Or if it isn't, Arnie Blassit would know it."

"Buddy, there's the chance that if we're right, and we get Lucas down here and find the place, it may be gone. If somebody overheard them talking, Jenna and Lucas, and figured they could find it themselves . . ."

"Then that would be the person who killed Jenna."

Alex made a slow ceremony of lighting a cigarette. He said quietly, "Has anybody thought of Donnie Capp?"

Buddy stared at him blankly. "Donnie?"

"Is there something sacred about him, for God's sake? Look at the facts. He was at the Mack. He sat with Jenna and Lucas during the tail end of their conversation. He patrolled the beach road often enough so it wouldn't mean anything if his car was seen out there. He's put on a hell of an act about finding out who did it. And he's been damned insistent about nobody prying into the case."

"Yes, but . . ."

"Try this for size, Buddy. He heard enough to know that Lucas could take him to some spot Jenna had described. He talked to Lucas after Jenna left the table. And it's possible that Jenna, drunk, wasn't as subtle as she thought she was being. So he left and waited for her, thinking about the money. Maybe he tried to make some kind of deal with her. She wanted no part of Donnie Capp. And so he killed her. And then he had it made. All he had to do was wait until it all died down, wait a month or so, and then get Lucas to take him to the place Jenna had described. Secretly. And it would have been no trick for him to kill Lucas, sink his body in a hole and leave his boat adrift. You know what people would have said. Then all he would have had to do was wait a little longer, think up some logical reason for quitting, and take off with the money. But he didn't count on Lucas's daughter coming after him and taking him away so suddenly. That left him in a bad spot. He couldn't go bring Lucas back without attracting a lot of unwelcome attention. And it made the murder of Jenna meaningless. I think he's under a hell of a strain. He doesn't know what to do. He's getting damned erratic. The way he worked me over is maybe an evidence of strain. Take it out on somebody, anybody."

"Donnie Capp," Buddy said softly. "On the job twenty-four hours a day, and he's never tried to graft a dime."

"But this is a lot more than a dime."

"Now here is a funny thing," Buddy said slowly. "Donnie has hunted all his life. He never gave a damn for fishing. About Christmas he came in and he bought himself a little twelve-foot aluminum boat and a big rebuilt outboard. Betty made him a good price, I remember. And we tried to tell him that motor was too big to troll good, but he said he didn't have much time and he'd rather run fast to where he was going, even if it did troll a little rough. And I tell you that most of the winter old Donnie was the fishingest man you'd ever want to see. He took a lot of kidding about it on account of he just never could come back in with much of anything. And finally Roy Lawlor got tired of trying to get hold of Donnie and not being able to get him, so he clamped down some. He still goes out a lot but not so often. Keeps the boat over there the other side of Bay Street, tied up at Garner's Bait Dock. You see him scoot out under the bridge every so often, with that big hat on him. He must sleep in that hat."

"So he's been trying to find it by himself."

"You go too damn far, Alex. There's no reason why a man can't take up fishing. And when a man takes it up, it can get to be a disease. And Donnie was a hunting fool until he took up fishing. I know Donnie pretty well, I just can't see him . . . killing my sister."

Alex thought for a few minutes. "If a man was going out hunting for that money, what would be the thing he'd most likely take with him?"

"Well, he'd take a shovel. Right after my father died, there was a run on shovels like you never see before."

"And he wouldn't be likely to carry a shovel to that boat every time he went out, would he?"

"It would look damn funny. I see what you mean. Let's go."

Buddy stuck his head in the office and told Betty they would be back in a little while. Buddy drove the blue jeep down Front Street and across Bay and another three blocks to Garner's. They walked out onto the dock.

"Here it is," he said. The aluminum boat was tied off, with a stern line on a piling, the bow line on a cleat on the dock. Buddy untied the bow line and brought the boat in close to a rotting step. He stepped into it lithely for a man of his size. Alex held the bow line and looked down into the boat. Buddy squatted and reached up under the shallow foredeck. He took out an object wrapped in a faded green tarp. He unwrapped it. They both stared at the folded entrenching tool for a few moments. Buddy wrapped it up again and stowed it. He climbed up onto the dock and was making the bow line fast when Alex turned and saw Donnie Capp walking swiftly toward them along the dock, his sallow face expressionless.

"What's goin' on?" he asked.

Buddy looked up at him casually. "Hi, Donnie. Alex here was thinking on getting a boat for himself. I told him about the rig we fixed you up with, and he wanted to see it, so I figured you wouldn't mind if I showed it to him."

"You have to get into it to show it to him?"

"Tell you the truth, Donnie, I forgot what horse motor you got, so I got in to lift up the motor cover and take a look."

"It's a little big for the boat," Alex said. "I think a ten would do me."

Buddy stood up and they stood facing Donnie Capp. The narrow colorless eyes swiveled quickly from face to face. Buddy said, "I guess it suits you all right, Donnie."

"It's fine."

"Have you got a good used ten-horse around?" Alex asked Buddy.

"We better go back and check with John Geer."

"If you got a boat like this one, why didn't you show

him the one you got instead of mine?" Donnie asked.

Buddy faltered for a moment and said, "Well, we haven't exactly got one, Donnie, but there's a fella has one wants to make a trade. And if we got a sale on the one he wants to trade, we can make him a better price. This time of year you have to get out and move the merchandise."

"How about letting me take it out?" Alex asked quickly.

Donnie stared at him. He turned and spat into the water. "If you was on fire, Doyle, I wouldn't do you the favor to push you off this here dock. And because you sold me the boat, Buddy, it doesn't give you any right to mess with it."

He turned on his heel and walked away. They could see the county car parked beside Garner's shack.

"I need a drink," Buddy said.

They parked the jeep in front of the Mack and went in. Janie was tending bar. They took a table far from the bar, over by the bowling machine. They both ordered beer and, as Janie turned away, Buddy asked her to bring a shot with his.

Buddy threw the shot down, gulped half the glass of beer and said, "I needed that. How did I do, talking to him?" He kept his voice low.

"I don't know. If I'm right, he's going to be suspicious of every damn thing."

"You made a hell of a good guess."

"Will you buy it?"

"I'll buy part of it, Alex. Somebody else could have killed her and all the rest of it could still be the way you say."

"I'll grant that. But suppose we were both sure he did kill her? What would we do next?"

"You couldn't find proof. There wasn't a clue. And I don't think he'd crack. If I was dead sure, Alex, I think I'd just up and kill him with my hands. Ever since I got my growth I've had to be careful about losing my temper.

I cleaned this place out one night. Over seven hundred bucks' damages. It was some crack somebody made about Betty. I didn't kill anybody. But I come too damn close for comfort. He was out cold for three days and he didn't get out of Davis General Hospital for nearly three weeks."

"That would be a dandy solution, Buddy. You kill him and the law takes care of you. Nice for Betty and your mother. But you've been the big hero, so it's all right."

"I talk a lot, don't I?"

"The thing to do is get hold of Lucas Pennyweather and get him down here. Pay his way. See if he can take you to the place Jenna described to him, if she did describe a specific place. It's worth the gamble. You've got a legitimate reason. And . . . it might be interesting to see how Capp reacts if Lucas shows up down here."

"Here comes Betty. Let's keep it to ourselves."

She came directly to the table and said, "Well! My spies reported the jeep in front of this place. If a girl wants a beer, she has to come get her own." She sat down. "One brew, Janie, please."

"Who's minding the store?" Buddy asked.

"The capable Mrs. West and the capable Mr. Geer. There was a phone call from Clearwater. Mr. Hitchins. He wants to have that Consolidated of his brought down here for a lot of work and summer storage. I said we could take it."

"Forty-two feet, isn't it?"

"With two Chrysler 275's. I looked it up. His captain will bring it down and turn it over to us. I guess you must have had an intensive tour of inspection, Alex."

"I saw everything. Saw the *Lady Bird*."

"My angel. Can I ask what is the matter with you two? Aren't you getting along? You act odd and strained."

"We're getting along fine, Betty."

She looked at the two of them dubiously. "I hope so."

They talked boats for a little while and then went back to the yard. Betty went into the office. Buddy stood by Alex beside the Dodge. "I'll get the address and get the call through. If he's well enough to come down, I'll pay his way. That is, if Jenna told him anything definite. I'll go over town now and find out the address and make the call."

Alex looked at his watch. "It's after four now. I want to stop and see Myra Ducklin. Why don't you bring Betty out for a swim later on and you can tell me how you made out?"

"Okay."

Doyle had a visit with Myra Ducklin. It was a little after five when he drove back toward the key. He thought of his own deductions, not with pride, but with grim and somewhat weary acceptance. A stranger could not have come to Ramona and found such an inevitable way of fitting the pieces together. And the local people had been too close to it all to understand how and why it had happened. It had required the rare combination of great familiarity so that people would talk, plus that special detachment which came from having been away so long. And perhaps one additional factor had been necessary— the sort of training which made you alert to the motives of other human beings, which taught you to turn odd facts this way and that way until a pattern began to form, until you began to sense what you had to look for to complete the pattern and make it so obvious that you began to wonder how it could have been overlooked.

He felt reasonably certain that Capp had killed the woman, had held her by the throat until she was dead. But one portion of the pattern was indistinct. He could not account for the odd reactions of Colonel M'Gann at the time he had talked to him. The curious reference to suicide. The man's insistence on staying here where this thing had happened.

The blue jeep was in his back yard. The house was

empty. He changed to trunks and went out onto the beach. They were swimming, a hundred yards off shore. Betty waved to him and he swam out to where they were.

chapter EIGHT

BUDDY MADE THE OPPORTUNITY to talk privately with Alex by saying, "Any obliging type gal would swim in and open up some cold beer that we brought out and put in your ice box, and be there on the beach to meet us when we come out."

"I just work here," she said, and made a face at them and swam toward the cottage.

Buddy rolled over on his back and floated. "Got the name and the town, but not the address. A Mrs. Trace Annison up in Fayetteville, North Carolina. Ran into Judge Ellandon outside of Ducklin's and he give me the name. So I got change and phoned up there. Got hold of her. Could hear a lot of kids squalling in the background. Funny damn thing, Alex, she thought I was phoning her to say Lucas had showed up down here. Couldn't get it through her head I wasn't phoning from the sheriff's office.

"She cried a little on the phone. Said Lucas had gotten real restless the past few months. Kept saying he was homesick for the sight of water. And about eight or nine days ago he took off. Left her a note saying he was coming back here. She knows he couldn't have had more than ten dollars on him, probably not that much. Soon as she found the note she phoned the sheriff's office over in Davis. She doesn't think Lucas is right in the head. And he's too old to be beating his way back across country. She asked Lawlor to keep a lookout for him and let her know by collect phone when he arrives so she can come back down and pick him up again."

"Then Lawlor would have told Donnie!"

"Sure he would. So Donnie is waiting for him."

"Where would Lucas head for when he gets back?"

"Depends on the time of day. If it was morning, I guess he'd head for Chaney's Bayou, back to that shack he shared with Arnie Blassit. And if it was afternoon or evening, he'd probably head for the Mack. You know, he must be awful close to eighty years old, Alex."

"I wouldn't want Donnie to get to him before anybody sees him. He might never be seen again."

"Just how the hell do you make sure that won't happen?"

"I don't know, Buddy."

"I know one thing. It isn't natural that if Donnie knew about it from Lawlor, he wouldn't pass the word around. People would get a kick out of it, old Lucas running out on his daughter and heading back here. It's the kind of thing you'd talk about."

"Have you told anybody about it?"

"Just you."

"Then wouldn't it help a little to spread the word? So people would be looking for him?"

Buddy asked then, in a quiet voice, "What if he already got here, Alex? How can we know he didn't make it back here fast? How can we know Donnie hasn't already got the money and Lucas is some place on the bottom of the bay?"

"That could have happened. He could have come in at night, walking over from Davis. Donnie must patrol that road."

"Right often. But, wait a minute—now you've got me doing it—how about that shovel? If Lucas found the place for him, it would be natural to leave that shovel there, wouldn't it? If he got it all, he wouldn't need the shovel. And if he wasn't sure he got it all, he'd leave it there for the next time he got a chance to go back and dig."

"So let's figure that Lucas hasn't gotten here yet. It's about all we can do."

"And I'll spread the word that he's on his way back, that he run away from home like a little kid."

"It will get back to Donnie."

"Sure it will, and it ought to give him the jumps. That is, Alex, if we haven't been going overboard with all this guesswork."

"You saw the shovel."

"I know. I know. And I saw how he acted this afternoon. But we seem to be getting spread so damn thin. I wish there was more to go on."

Alex heard Betty's shout and looked toward the beach. She was standing holding two cans of beer aloft. They swam in, side by side. When they walked up the slant of the beach together, Alex sensed that Buddy's great hard bulk must make him look almost frail in comparison.

Later, when Betty had gone to shower and change, Buddy said, "Got me another idea, Alex."

"Yes?"

"If Lucas comes in and he gets him, he'd use his own boat. Might have to leave Lucas tied up some place along the shore line where nobody would run across him before Donnie came to get him in that boat. So I can fix that boat a little. Easiest way is to plug the cooling system. He wouldn't notice anything wrong. He'd go a couple of miles before it quit cold on him. Do that tonight."

"Be careful."

"I can move quiet in the dark."

They left at six-thirty. Doyle sat on his porch and watched the last of the sunset. Just as the light was fading, a figure came into his line of vision, coming from his right, walking hastily along the packed sand at the water's edge, almost running. He recognized Celia M'Gann, and there was such a look of trouble in the way she moved that he got up and went out into the gathering night. The screen door slammed behind him.

She stopped at the sound and took several tentative steps toward the cottage. "Mr. Doyle?" Her voice was shrill and taut, as though she could be close to losing control.

"Yes, Miss M'Gann," he said, walking toward her.

"Have you seen my brother? Have you seen the colonel?"

"No, I haven't."

"Have you been here long?"

"Since a little after five. I guess I would have seen him if he went by on the beach. I wasn't watching the road."

"Could you . . . help me look for him?"

"Sure. What's wrong?"

And suddenly she was crying silently. There was just enough light in the west so that he could see her face, contorted like a child's, as she stood there with her fists tightly clenched.

"You better try to tell me what's wrong," he said softly. And, to his discomfiture and astonishment, she turned and thrust herself against him, sobbing in a hoarse and rasping way against his throat, her strong body shaking. It did not last long. She wrenched herself away, saying harshly, "How stupid! How damn girlish!"

"Can you tell me what's wrong?"

She stood with her back to him, wearing a pale blouse and a dark skirt, sandaled feet planted strongly on the tide-wet sand. She made a half gesture toward the charcoal Gulf. "He . . . might be out there."

"And he might not be out there. He could have taken a walk."

"Not after what happened."

"What did happen? If you tell me maybe I can be more help to you."

She turned and it was now too dark for him to see

her expression. "You seem to be speaking with a good deal more precision, Mr. Doyle. What did you say to him when I left you alone?"

"I don't know what you mean."

"Something changed him. I'm supposed to be an administrator, Mr. Doyle. I am on a leave of absence from a large insurance company. I was in charge of a section employing over three hundred women. I'm not a fool. I'm not as brilliant as my brother but I'm no fool. I could handle those women adequately. Today I said the wrong thing. I said a stupid thing. If he's gone, it's my fault. We're twins. We've always been close. We've always had a curious awareness of what the other one is thinking. I do not see how I could have gone six months without knowing what was in his mind and how it was affecting him, holding him back when he should have been improving."

She took a half step closer to him. "He didn't take his nap today. He sat on the porch, almost motionless. I made his highball at five o'clock and took it to him. I sat by him, doing some mending. Without any warning at all, he said, 'Did you kill her, Celia?' What should my reaction have been? I know now. I should have reacted violently, with a horror, dismay that he could think such a thing. So, in complete stupidity, I sat there and said in a sort of mild and chiding way, 'What a strange idea, Crawford. Of course not!' And he did not speak again. And about fifteen minutes ago I found he was gone. For six months he's been thinking I killed her. I know that now. It explains how he's acted."

Her fingers suddenly closed around his wrist. They were cold and strong. "So now he must think I did. And what could he do with a conviction like that? Turn me in? Keep on letting me take care of him? Live with that knowledge? An almost insoluble problem for the kind of man he is. I reacted improperly, Mr. Doyle, because you become accustomed to treating invalids as if they were children. And because I am guilty. I came so horribly close to killing her. So desperately close. I should have told him. But I didn't want to risk upsetting him even more than he was already upset when he learned she was dead. He wasn't as strong six months ago as he is now. And after a little while . . . it seemed too late. But he must have heard me leave the cottage that night. And return. And he never let on that he had heard anything. He's always known there wasn't anything in the world I wouldn't do for him. And I almost did him the . . . ultimate favor. Help me, Mr. Doyle. Help me find him."

He went out to the car and got a flashlight out of the glove compartment. He walked up the beach with her. The tide was coming in. The waves had already erased the tracks she had made walking down toward his cottage. He could find no sign of any tracks the colonel might have left.

They walked north. As they walked she said, "I have the feeling it's ended now. All of it. She was such a horror. I was afraid the cumulative strain of her misbehavior would kill him. Every time she didn't return for two or three nights, I would be hoping she'd never come back. We had a terrible quarrel out on the beach the Wednesday before she was killed. I tried to plead with her, to beg her to be considerate. I couldn't reach her. She told me to live my own life, not hers. I said that I shouldn't have expected more of her. She had come from nothing. And then she started to curse and rant at me, telling me how good her family was, how her father had been a wealthy man, how he had bought her everything. And she brought up that ridiculous myth of hidden money.

"I told her that when a hard, shrewd man lived in a small town and made a fetish of secrecy, rumor always credited him with a fortune he didn't have. Instead of a mythical fortune, it would have been far better, I said, if he had left her a legacy of decency and manners. She started to tell me, violently, how nice her dear daddy had been to her when she was little. And quite suddenly she stopped. She looked as if she had quite forgotten I was there. When I spoke to her she stared at me as if she didn't know my name, and turned and walked away."

Celia M'Gann was talking tensely and rapidly, with a threat of hysteria in her voice. He sensed that it was compulsive talking, a device she was using to hold herself together.

"I worried about the quarrel, Mr. Doyle. I felt I had handled her wrong. Better if I had tried to bribe her to put less strain on my brother. She was a greedy little thing. I didn't get a chance to try a new tack on Thursday or Friday. I couldn't sleep Friday night. I knew her habits. Many times she had walked back from town alone, along the beach, because the walking was better and there were fewer mosquitoes on the open beach. It was more probable that she would have a date, and then there would be no telling when she would come rolling in. But, because I couldn't sleep with the problem on my mind, it seemed worth taking a chance of meeting her. I got up very quietly, and left the cottage. It was a little after two. Even if I missed her, I thought the walk would help.

"I met her not far beyond the cottage where you are. She was quite unsteady, but she was coherent. She was surprised to see me. There was a little moonlight. We stood there and I tried to reason with her. If all else failed, I was going to offer her all my savings to leave and never come back. It's an . . . adequate amount. She teetered and leered at me there in the moonlight and then in the most foul possible way she hinted at . . . an unspeakable relationship between my brother and myself. She tried to soil the finest thing in my life. I do not know exactly what happened. It was as though I went blind and numb. When sensation came back I was standing over her. She lay unconscious on the sand, and I had a terrible blazing pain in my clenched fist. I had never struck anybody with my fist before. I'm a strong woman. I had noticed the tide was coming in. I bent over her and thought of dragging her into the water. I tried but I could not force myself to touch her. Then I saw that the tide would reach her before very long. I turned and ran, literally ran back to our cottage. I sank exhausted on the sand, trembling, nauseated.

"In a little while I knew it was something I could not do. I could not leave her there. No matter how dangerous she was to my brother, I could not kill. And so I went back. I stopped just about in front of your cottage when I saw, far off in the moonlight, somebody bending over her. I could not tell if it was a man or a woman. I knew she would be all right. It was even possible she wouldn't remember me striking her. And so I went back to bed and stayed awake waiting for her to come in. She was always noisy when she came in. She had no consideration. None. I fell asleep. And we were both awakened by that Darcey woman, screaming and gibbering outside the cottage."

"You haven't told anyone this."

"No. What good would it have done to subject myself to a lot of clumsy interrogation? I couldn't possibly identify the person I had seen with her. And she had died of strangulation, not drowning. I suppose in a certain sense I did contribute to her death."

"Do you think you were seen by the person who killed her? He could have been following her, or waiting to intercept her."

"I thought of that. I worried about it. But he could not have told of seeing me without implicating himself. Unless he were caught, and then there was the chance he would try to blame it all on me. That was a risk I had to take. And, you know, I could not be at all certain I had been seen. When I woke up, my hand was badly puffed. I pretended to burn it when I fixed breakfast. It gave me a chance to bandage it so the puffiness did not

show. It did not last long. And now . . . it all ends
this way. And all for nothing. Because I tried to save
him."

They were far beyond the Proctor cottage, and beyond
where the road ended at the Janson land.

Doyle had been shining the flashlight on the smooth
unmarked sand. And suddenly he picked up the indentation of a naked foot, and another, walking away from
the water. She clutched his arm. She looked at the empty
beach and toward the blackness of the brush.

"Crawford!" she called, her voice wild and lost in the
emptiness of the night. "Crawford!"

"I'm right here," he said, so close that it startled
both of them. Doyle turned his light toward the shadows.
Colonel M'Gann sat slumped on the sand, his back
against the bole of a big Australian pine that had been
brought down by erosion. Celia ran to him and dropped
to her knees in the sand and, with a strange harsh cry
of pain and gladness, put her arms around him. Doyle
turned the light away from them. The woman was sobbing
quietly.

M'Gann said, apparently addressing Doyle, ignoring his
sister, "The survival instinct is a strong and curious thing.
I walked up this way and swam out beyond my limit.
I knew it was beyond my strength to get back. And at
the first edge of panic, the brute body took over, pac-
ing itself, struggling to live. The heart should have quit,
but it didn't. And so I lay in the shallows finally, until
I had the strength to get up."

"She has something to tell you, Colonel."

"I know what she has to tell me."

"I don't think you do."

Doyle went up the beach. The murmur of her voice
faded away. He waited a long time. Finally Celia called
him and he walked back to them.

"I guess I've been a fool," the colonel said.

"We . . . I think I know who killed her."

"Can you tell us? Not that it matters terribly," he said.

"Not yet. If we can't prove it somehow, I'll tell you."

"Mr. Doyle, my sister's protective instinct toward me has always been obsessive. She has had so little emotional release in her own life that her concern has not been entirely . . . healthy. Hush, Celia, please. Jenna's behavior was hampering my recovery. I heard Celia go out and I heard her come back, but I lied to the sheriff, as she did. And I let myself believe she had done something I should have known her to be incapable of. I'm ashamed of that. I decided to call it justifiable homicide. Be her judge and jury. But I would find myself looking at her hands and thinking of how Jenna had been when we were first married. I thought I knew what she was keeping from me. Early this evening I finally tested her. From the way she answered, I knew I could no longer afford the small luxury of doubt. And my solution seemed to me to be . . . apt. As I told you, Mr. Doyle, I was faced with an emotional problem. An ethical problem."

"Why would you say that to him?" Celia asked.

"Colonel, what can I tell Colonel Presser now?"

"I don't know yet. I have to adjust to . . . new knowledge. And I will have to find out what damage was done by this . . . asinine little adventure of mine. God help the man who takes himself so seriously, Mr. Doyle."

"What is this talk about Colonel Presser?" Celia demanded. "Has this Mr. Doyle sneaked around my back and . . ."

"Please be still, Celia. Mr. Doyle is a very competent and effective man. Mr. Doyle, it would be inefficient to keep you here while I make one of my slow decisions. Mission accomplished, I would say. There's no more you can do. You can tell Austin that I will be in touch with him in a week or two. If I say yes, and I think I might, he could then send some people down here to bring me up to date."

Celia had jumped to her feet. "I will *not* have it! You

are *not* going to go back and let them work you to death. You're a sick man and I will not . . ."

"Celia!" he roared.

"But . . ." she said in a small voice.

"You will order the lives of those female clerks of yours, but you will not order my life for me. I am grateful for your care. It does not give you the authority you seem to think is yours. My apologies, Mr. Doyle. Family scene."

"Can I help you back to the cottage?"

"No thanks. I'll rest a little longer. And then Celia can help me if necessary. I suppose you'll be going back now?"

"Not yet, Colonel. One mission accomplished. The official one. And now there's a personal one. It seems to be . . . necessary. Miss M'Gann, could I ask you one question?"

"After you lied to me about . . ."

"My sister will answer your question, Mr. Doyle. She'll remember later she has reasons to be grateful to you, and she'll regret her rudeness."

"You said you were too far to identify the person you saw bending over Jenna."

"That's right."

"Was there any distinguishing thing at all? Light clothing or dark clothing?"

"I was much too far away, in that light. But . . . I got the impression that the figure was wearing a beach hat. One of those straw things, like a coolie hat. It somehow gave me the impression that it was a woman, but it seemed strange for her to be wearing it at night."

"Do you recall Deputy Capp's hat?"

"Of course. That Texas-looking thing. I see what you mean. I couldn't swear to it. But at that distance that cream-colored hat could have given me that impression. You must realize that had I known I was seeing a murderer, I would have been more observing."

"Thank you. And good night. If there's anything I can do . . ."

"We're all right now," the colonel said. They both said good night to him. He walked back to his cottage. Now the pattern was more distinct. The blurred area was gone. Donnie Capp had bent over the unconscious woman. Perhaps he, too, had thought of pushing her into the water. And then she had begun to stir. And before she was conscious enough to fight him, he had closed that small, sallow, wiry hand around her throat. Maybe it had not been premeditated. Maybe her very helplessness had triggered a new aspect of that deep sadistic aspect of him.

He knew it was not yet finished here for him. Now that he was free to leave, he could not. It was not revenge against Donnie, or the desire to protect Lucas, or even the strange enchantment of the handsome and unapproachable girl. It was part of being home again. As though, by accomplishing something difficult and perhaps dangerous, he could pay in partial measure for the long years of exile, self-imposed.

As he ate and as he showered and as he lay sleepless in a slant of April moonlight, he thought of Donnie Capp.

chapter NINE

SATURDAY was a strange day. The sun shone through a mist that would not burn away. The Gulf had a silvery, milky look, a shining calm, yet with a swell that lifted slowly, sleekly to break finally after long hesitation against the sand—like long-spaced recurrent sighs. The terns swooped and yelped in an unknown excitement, and Doyle could not see where the sea joined the sky at the distant horizon. He stood on the beach and saw something he had never seen as a child or as a young man.

Five hundred feet from shore a giant ray—a devil fish —burst up through the pearly surface and seemed to hang for one incredible moment suspended, as black as evil, between sea and sky before falling with its hundreds of pounds of weight, cracking its great wings against the water surface with a sound that had a sharp echoing resonance. The look of it gave him a crawling, shuddering sensation, a special awareness of his own mortality.

At mid-morning he drove over into the town to the boat yard. Buddy said secretively that he had plugged the cooling system on Donnie's motor without being seen, and that he had told enough people about the expected return of Lucas to be assured that the news would spread quickly. He had seen Donnie Capp's car parked on Bay Street earlier in the morning, but he had not seen Donnie.

They stood talking at the far end of the work shed. Buddy said, "I don't hardly ever dream. But I dreamed last night about Donnie. And today it seems more like he could have done it. Funny, isn't it? But . . . this is the kind of a day I guess when it's easier to think of people killing people. Line storms out in the Gulf. We ought to get weather before the day's over."

"Nothing to do now but wait."

"I stopped in the Mack last night. Arnie Blassit came in. Told him that if Lucas showed up to bring him right to me fast as he could make it. He wanted to know why. I told him I'd tell him why later on, that it was important. Told him to keep his mouth shut about it."

Betty came toward them. "Now what's going on? Are you people forming some kind of a secret club? Maybe you should build a nice tree house for meetings. Alex, did you see my watch?"

"No."

"I keep looking at my empty wrist. I left it on that little shelf near your outside shower stall. Very stupid of me. I can see it sitting there, just as plain. I don't want it to get rained on."

"I'll go get it right away."

"Would you, please?" She walked to where she could get a better look at the sky. "On second thought, it isn't going to rain right away. John has gone off in the jeep. This whole place is dead as a tomb. And a day like this makes me feel stickier and restlesser than a real hot one. Brother, dear, I think I'll goof off and take a short swim and pick up my watch and let Alex take me to lunch in something air-conditioned. And I will slave like a dog all afternoon to make up. Why don't you come too?"

"I've got to get Marty's boat ready. He's picking it up at twelve-thirty. We can't all goof off around here."

Alex waited a few minutes for Betty in front of the office and then they got into the old Dodge and he drove back toward the beach. She looked slightly wilted. The bridge timbers rumbled under the wheels. After the bridge there was a short stretch of causeway, and then a sharp right-hand turn onto the narrow key road, a turn made almost blind by a big tangle of palmetto and yucca at the corner.

Just as he reached the turn he caught a glimpse of something through the mass of foliage, something big and fast —and heard the hard high roar of a truck moving fast in low gear. He knew at once that if he tried to make the turn, he would turn right into it. If he tried to stop, his momentum would take him across its bows and he would be smashed broadside. With both luck and instinct, he took the only course possible. He swung the wheel hard left and stamped on the gas to swing the rear end around, knowing that if the truck tried to make the turn onto the causeway instead of continuing south on the key road, it would smash into him.

The truck was upon them, and for a frozen moment the blunt bow of the big dusty GMC seemed to hang over them. But then the sliding turn pulled his hood away.

For one microsecond they were side by side, both headed in the same direction. And then his right rear corner, still sliding, slammed into the big rear duals of the truck, bounced away so violently that the Dodge hung for a moment on the verge of going over, came down with a force that burst a tire, and wobbled crazily into the ditch, the wide and shallow ditch on the other side of the road, the car aimed back toward the bridge and the causeway. He turned off the engine and they could hear the roar of the truck receding south in the distance.

They stared at each other. She looked sick under her tan. "Absolutely insane!" she said.

"Who was it?"

"I haven't the faintest. But he's still on the key, and this is the only way off. Drunk, I'd say. Alex, you did a perfectly wonderful job!"

"Thanks." He took out cigarettes, gave her one. When he tried to light hers, they had difficulty getting the flame and the cigarette end together until she grinned at him and held his wrist.

"I'd get out," he said, "if I was sure my knees would work."

"You'll have to get out first. It's all bayonets on my side."

He got out onto the sand road and she got out and stood beside him. Except for the constant metallic song of insects in the brush, the morning was breathlessly still.

"I'll have to run it forward and up out of the ditch before I can change that tire," he said.

"Listen!"

He heard the truck sound again, as faint as the shrilling of the insects, but growing louder as it came toward them.

"We should flag that maniac down!" she said. "At least we'll find out who he is so it can be reported."

"Get back in the ditch, Betty, out of the way. We don't know how drunk he is."

She moved into the ditch behind the car. He stood out beside the car. In a moment he could see the truck, and he heard the motor sound change as it slowed to make the turn into town. He began waving his arm in a big arc, palm down, trying to flag the truck down. He saw the big hood and a face behind the window of the cab and, with a feeling of incredulity, he saw the big wheels cut toward him. He whirled and dived headlong across the left front fender of the Dodge, banging his right knee sharply on the fender. He hit on his shoulder in the ditch and rolled into a thousand knives. And looked just in time to see the truck bounce high as it hit the crown of the wooden bridge and continue at high speed toward the foot of Bay Street.

He sat and hugged his leg, grimacing with pain. Betty ran to him, her eyes wild and her mouth working.

"Did he hit you?"

Pain made him irritable. "Yes. He hit me square and killed me dead, for God's sake."

"I'm sorry. I couldn't see. He came so close."

"Help me get up so I can walk on this thing."

She took his hand and pulled him up. He limped around in a small circle and felt the pain diminish. In a very few moments he could put all his weight on the leg without wincing. He looked at the dual tracks in the hard sand and shell surface. The truck had barely missed the car, and the duals had run well inside where he had been standing.

"He swerved at you," she said.

"I know."

"Alex, there's spots of blood on the back of your shirt!"

"I rolled into those bayonets."

"You know, it was a County Road Department truck. And it was one of the Kemmer boys driving. I can't remember his name."

"Lee?"

"Yes! That's the one. Did you see him?"

"I was too busy both times he went by."

He started the car and ran it at an angle out of the ditch on the flat right rear. He changed to the bald-headed spare, collapsed the jack, put the burst tire in the trunk.

"You're so quiet about it," Betty said.

"Right after we got across the bridge I thought I heard a motor start up. I think I know where it could have been. Let's go take a look."

She got in and he got the car turned around. He drove two hundred yards and stopped on the right shoulder and got out. She followed him. He crossed the road and turned and looked toward the bridge. He remembered having noticed that from that spot you could see the crown of the bridge and a segment of the causeway.

A truck had been backed into the brush on the west side of the road at that point where the view was best. He sat on his heels and when she came up behind him, he pointed with a twig at drops of fresh, shiny, black oil on a green leaf. He guessed where the cab door would have been, and found four fresh cigarette butts near by. A wink of glass in the brush caught his eye. He picked it up. An uncapped and empty pint bottle that had held a cheap blend. He smelled it. The whisky odor was sharp and fresh.

"Do you think he was waiting here? I mean . . . waiting until you . . ."

"It's a funny place to park. He was going like hell in a low gear when he hit the corner. And when he came back, he tried again." He threw the bottle aside.

"How about fingerprints on the bottle? It's attempted murder, isn't it?"

"He missed. So it's drunken driving, if you can prove it, or reckless driving, and that would have to be proven too. And if you could grab that Kemmer character and try to beat it out of him, he wouldn't know what the hell you were talking about, because he has first-hand knowledge of just what Donnie can do with that club. Let's get that swim."

"I guess any of those Kemmers would do just what Donnie said. But do you really think Donnie would tell him to kill you?"

"Donnie doesn't like me. Not at all. And you could hardly believe he'd work me over. When a man gets into the habit of thinking he can get away with anything, it isn't much of a jump from a clubbing to a killing."

"There's something going on I don't know about."

"Let's get that swim."

"But if somebody is really trying to kill you, it wouldn't be safe to go and swim, would it?"

"It might not be too safe for me to go swimming alone. I don't know. Lee Kemmer has got to report that it didn't work. Suppose it had worked, and I'd been alone in the car. Donnie could come up with witnesses, some of his tame rabbits willing to swear I'd swerved right into the path of the truck. Too bad. Nobody to get indignant about Alex Doyle, transient."

"I would!"

"But if it hadn't gone sour, he'd have killed both of us, Betty. And that would be more of a stink than Donnie is prepared to face. He can be thankful Lee Kemmer missed. He couldn't have seen there was somebody in the car with me. They'll have to cook up something else, involving me alone. So it's safe to swim. I'm safe when I'm with you. Come on."

They went to the cottage. When he was in his trunks she inspected his back, and went and found the dark dregs of a bottle of iodine and dabbed each puncture. They swam together. A line of green-black had crept up from the southwest horizon, extending all the way across the sky. The swells were heavier and slower, and an infrequent gust of wind would scamper and swirl across the water before dying away.

She sat beside him on the old blanket on the beach, subdued and thoughtful, hugging her knees, while they watched the slow approach of the distant storm. She shuddered suddenly.

"Cold?"

"No. Delayed reaction, I guess. Thinking about how it could have been if you hadn't been so quick. I didn't know what was happening. I would have run right into him."

"It didn't happen."

"Alex?"

"Yes, Miss Betty."

"Everything seems to be changing for me. Since you've come back."

"How?"

"Oh, I had a nice clean tidy little shell. Like a lady hermit crab. I was very comfortable, really. Nothing touched me. Now I'm part way out of my nice shell and I feel sort of . . . soft and naked and defenseless. And uncertain about things."

"My apologies."

"Now don't apologize. I'm more alive, I guess. More aware of the people around me. And their motives. I felt all perfectly adjusted forever and ever, and pretty smug about myself. And now my tender little psyche is hanging out in the cold wind. Maybe it's a kind of discontent. I don't know. I want to back into my shell again, but it doesn't seem to fit." She turned and looked at him. "Have you ever had a bad fever?"

"Yes."

"Do you remember how . . . painful things look? I mean so sharp and clear. And even simple things take on sort of ominous personalities. And sounds are so vivid you want to cover your ears. This is a cousin of that."

"Listen, Betty. Here it comes."

They listened to the oncoming roar of the rain. He

folded the blanket and they walked to the cottage. He put the blanket inside and went out onto the porch just as it hit. She stood on white sand thirty feet in front of the cottage in a dark red suit, erect, her brown shoulders back, her face tilted toward the sky, standing in a curious green light outlined for moments against the onrushing steaming curtain of rain, and the constant flare of lightning beyond it before the rain misted and obscured her. He felt that he had never seen anything quite as primitive and beautiful.

Soon the wind began to slant the cold rain, driving it in onto the porch. The day was darker, the lightning closer, and he could barely hear the thunder above the hammering roar of the rain on the roof. He retreated into the living room and moments later she came hurrying in, panting and gasping, her riotous hair plastered meekly against the good lines of her skull.

"It's a glorious storm!" she called to him over the rain roar. "It's wonderful!"

She borrowed his bedroom and closed the door and came out a little while later in her yellow blouse and white skirt, barefoot, hair in a white towel turban, her eyes still dancing with the excitement of the storm. The turmoil of the storm seemed to increase. The cottage creaked and stirred as the wind shouldered it. Whips of rain slashed the roof and windows. And, between the intensities of rain, all the world was a deep aquarium green. He went in and changed to dry khaki shorts and a T-shirt and then they stood close and looked out at the storm, and spoke loudly above the noise. When there was a rift they could see the Gulf, tilting hills of shining slate, foaming cream-white as it broke.

She turned on the kitchen light and made sandwiches and coffee. Just as they finished the lunch, the storm ended with astonishing abruptness, and went fading, bumbling, grumbling off into the east. And the world stayed dark.

"Come on," she said, and they went out onto the beach where the surf roared. The rain had smashed the sand flat, washed it clean. Their bare feet, male and female, made the first tracks seen on the planet. And, without self-consciousness, she took his hand as they walked.

"Here comes more!" she cried, and they ran back to the cottage just in time. The rain was not as heavy as before, but the wind was strong, the lightning more vivid and continual.

Suddenly there was a vivid and alarming clink of lightning, a white and blinding flash and simultaneous concentrated bang of thunder. The kitchen light went out. He could feel a numbed tingling in his hands and feet and he heard nervousness in her laugh. "I like it, but not that close."

He smiled down at her. Her face changed, illuminated there in the gloom by the dance of lightning, a sudden and solemn heaviness of eyes and lips, a tentative, searching look.

"Before . . . on the beach before the storm . . . I was trying to say something. Trying to hint, I guess. I don't know."

"Are you sure?"

"No, I'm not sure. I'm scared half out of my mind. So hurry, darling, before I turn and run. Try. Quickly."

He took her in his arms and kissed her. He felt the uncompromising rigidity of her lips, the slow stiffening of her body. He released her. She went over and sat on the shabby couch and turned her face away, sitting very still. They heard the last fragment of the storm move away.

"Damn," she said wearily. "All twisted up inside. Emotional cripple. False courage from a little lightning and wind. Sorry I inflicted myself on you. And now I won't be able to be . . . easy with you any more. So that's spoiled too. New element added."

"We'll just make out like it didn't happen."

More light was coming into the world. She looked at him with a strange and frightened defiance. "Maybe I should be forced."

"That's a bad idea."

"How do you know?"

"I don't, really. I just have a hunch it would be the worst thing that could happen to you."

She stood up. "The lady is neuter gender." She took off the turban and fluffed her hair. "Better drive it back to work, sir."

He stepped toward her, tilted her chin up, saw the quick alarm in her eyes, and sensed the effort she had to make to keep from twisting away from him. He kissed her very quickly and lightly on the lips.

"That's for affection, Miss Betty."

She smiled a small heartbreak and said, "That one didn't hurt a bit. Very fatherless. I mean fatherly . . . That was a funny slip of the lip. Probably significant. Without that deep therapy, I'll never know."

"I think one small thing would help. I think it might help a lot if you kept in mind at all times the fact that you are a very, very exciting woman. With a hell of a figure. With considerable loveliness. So walk proud, and think about that once in a while."

There was a red flush under her tan. "You're out of your mind! I'm a big husky horse."

"Ask around. Take a poll. It will check out."

"Jenna was dainty. And lovely."

"With an empty little teasing face and a practiced waggle of hips and the soul of a harpy. She was pretty in a shallow and provocative way. No more than that. And no more talk about it. Off we go."

On the way over to town she said, "Buddy will be frantic when he hears about that truck."

"I'd rather you wouldn't tell him."

"But why not!"

He parked in the small lot near her office, turned to face her, lit their cigarettes. "You keep saying, Betty, you think something is going on you don't know about. Something is. It isn't very pretty and there are no definite plans in effect right now. We're just waiting for something to happen. If it works right, you'll be told the whole thing. I'm used to waiting. And watching. Buddy isn't. I want him to be patient. If you tell him about the truck, he may do something impulsive. And dangerous to him."

"Now that I know there *is* something going on, I can get it out of him. He can't keep secrets from me."

"I'd rather you wouldn't try."

"All right. I won't try if you don't want me to. And I won't mention the truck. I will be the helpless female if that's what you want. I'll learn to simper."

"That should be enchanting."

"But for goodness sake, when you can tell me what you two are plotting, don't delay it."

She paused in the office doorway and waved to him and went in. He turned around and drove slowly down Front Street.

Donnie's official car was parked across from the Mack, empty. On impulse, Alex parked and went in. Donnie was at the bar alone, having a beer. Four men were at one table, talking baseball. Two noisy couples were at another table. Two men were playing the bowling machine. Janie was working the bar. It was only two-thirty, but the Mack was getting its usual start on Saturday night.

Alex went over and stood beside Donnie and said, "Storm cleared the air."

"Isn't so sticky now."

"Something I wanted to report, Mr. Deputy, sir."

Donnie turned his head slowly and looked up at him. "Keep talking."

"One of those Kemmer boys was running around

drunk in a county truck a couple of hours ago. Came right out at me. He could have run me down and killed me dead the way he was going, but at the last minute he turned the wheel and swerved around me."

"Too bad he missed," Donnie said casually, but Alex saw the little twitch of surprise and anger in the shallow eyes.

"So I've done my duty as a citizen, Mister Deputy, sir."

"If I see him one of these days I'll go out of my way to tell him to take it easy."

"Thank you, Mister Deputy, sir. Now maybe you'd answer a point of law. You remember putting knots on my head, I suppose."

"Enjoyed every minute of it. Hope you did."

"Now suppose while I was there helpless, Mister Deputy, sir, somebody else came in after you left and killed me dead? Would you be guilty of murder too?"

There was no expression on Capp's face, no slight flaw in the utter blankness as the long seconds passed. Alex tried to look composed and casual, but it was becoming a constantly greater effort.

"Now that's a right strange question to ask a man," Capp said softly.

"I just wondered about it. Idle curiosity, sir."

"It kills cats." Capp stood up. He pushed the club so it swung on the thong and thumped the front of the bar. "This is the only law I know, Doyle. Only kind I understand. Probably the only kind you understand too, come right down to it."

He pushed by Alex and went out, drove off through the dwindling rain puddles. Alex went out and stood by the car. He felt the familiar tensions of the chase, a taste in the back of his throat of a breathless expectancy. It was, in a sense, a dreadful art, this manipulation of human beings. Discover the area of stress. And then nudge so gently and so carefully. Back up the lions with a kitchen chair. But it had to be done delicately.

He remembered the embassy clerk in Madrid, the wide-faced, smiling fellow whose outgoing reports they had finally intercepted, written in code in a tiny hand on paper of a curious shade of pink. After they had made certain that he would have access to nothing more of any importance, they had searched until they found identical paper. And then, with great care, they had begun to plant strips of it in places where he would come across it. Those who think themselves monstrously clever can best be awed and broken by a phenomenon that can only be the result of greater cleverness. And by something they do not quite understand. It had been the intent to humble the smiling one until, by the time he was interrogated, he would be cooperative.

They watched the changes in him as the weeks went by, the new nervousness of the smile, the increasing intervals of inattention, a suggestion of a stammer, a slight facial tic, a weight loss. They were ready for him if he tried to run. The final strip of pink paper was planted with diabolical efficiency and perfect timing between the inner pages of the newspaper he usually purchased on his way from the embassy to his hotel. In order to guarantee success, slips had to be placed inside a hundred issues of the paper. To other purchasers they would be meaningless. But he could not help but think that his was the only copy containing such a slip, and he could not of course understand how, with such busy traffic at the newsstand, it had been managed. Two hours after he entered the hotel, one of those watching him saw him dive from the wide windows to the cobblestones four stories below, and swore later that he had seen a wide, idiot smile in the light of the street lamp as the man fell.

And that had been a mistake, of course. Too strong an attack on the area of strain, so that the subject had broken. A Donnie Capp could resist greater pressure. Now he sensed that he was suspect. He would know of the slow crumbling of his position of strength. The inspection of the boat. The circulation of the gossip about the return of Lucas. And, finally, this unmistakable hint that it was known that the person who had struck Jenna and the person who had strangled her were not the same. Until that moment, Capp would have been certain that only he and the one who struck the blow would have known of that strange division of effort.

Doyle wondered if he had pushed Capp a little too far. The man was capable of murder. He tried to guess what Capp's action would be. He had, perhaps, three choices. He could give up any thought of the money and content himself with the knowledge that the murder could not be proven. Yet he could not be entirely sure it could not be proven. Or he could gamble on being the first to find Lucas and make him lead him to the money and then run with it. Or he could, if bold enough, attempt in some safe way to eliminate the people who now seemed suspicious of him. He would know that included Doyle, Buddy Larkin and perhaps Betty Larkin. But he could not be certain if others had been told, or how much was known—how much they could have been told.

Doyle made his guess based on an appraisal of Capp's nature. The man was direct and brutal, but not essentially clever. Had he been clever he would not have been so impatient. He would have let Lucas help Jenna find the money, or find that there was no money. And if the money had been there, he could have begun his own action from that point. So, considering the factor of impatience, if Lucas had not yet finished his journey, the waiting would be difficult for Capp. And he would feel easier taking some sort of action, no matter how dangerous, than merely waiting. The more he thought of it, the more convinced he became that Capp was now highly dangerous—the lion grown contemptuous of the kitchen chair and the noisy blanks.

And so he drove back through the washed air, under the deep blue afternoon sky, and talked again with Buddy Larkin. He told Buddy that he had every intention of taking care of himself, and he would feel much better if Buddy made it his business to exercise the same care for both himself and Betty.

Buddy was mildly incredulous.

"Listen," Alex said, "your good old familiar Donnie is like a lighted fuse. If Lawlor wasn't the big thick-headed exhibitionist he is, if I could be sure he'd listen, I'd go talk to him. But we've got a hell of an involved chain of deduction. Too many ifs in it. If we had a little more evidence, I'd try to get him locked up."

"It's because he beat you up, Alex. You're jumpy."

"I'll tell you something you don't know, if you promise not to take any action whatsoever—except to be careful."

"What is it?"

"Promise first. It may sound childish, but promise first."

Buddy did. Alex told him of the truck and the narrowness of his and Betty's escape. And he told him why he had told Betty not to tell him. "Because I was afraid you'd turn into a wild man and get yourself in trouble and mess up any chances we have of trapping Capp."

Buddy, with iron face, turned slowly and smacked a stone fist against the shed wall. A pair of nippers ten feet away bounced off a hook and clanged on the slab floor.

"If he had . . ."

"Settle down! Do you still think it's stupid to use a little care?"

"No! Christ! I think he's gone crazy."

"He hasn't gone crazy, Buddy."

"No?"

"No. He went over the edge six months ago. And this whole town is to blame. You lawful people didn't care if he whipped heads just so long as he whipped the heads on the people who had no way of fighting back. You were even kind of sneaky proud of him. Toughest deputy on the west coast of Florida. And you thought that Old West outfit of his was amusing. You folks grew yourself a paranoid. Nobody has told me, but I can tell you just how he lives. He has a small place somewhere. With a lot of privacy. And he keeps it as bare and neat as a monk's cell. He'll have a gun rack and he'll keep those guns in perfect shape. He'll scrub the floor on his hands and knees. After he makes his bed, you can bounce a coin on it. No books, no television, no hobby except the guns and hunting. Nobody will ever drop in on him. When he wants a woman he'll go after one that's drab and humble and scared, and it will be as close to rape as the law allows."

"You're so damn right, Alex. How did you know about that?"

"I've seen so many of them. In the army, mostly."

"I never thought of it before, but there was a guy like that in my outfit. BAR man. God, he kept that thing in shape. He could do a sniper's job with it. Never had a word for anybody. Neatest damn marine I ever saw. Sneak out at night by himself and come back with gook hardware. A killer. Volunteer for every patrol. He finally bought it, but he sure had a lopsided score before he did. He cost them. Donnie has a little cinderblock place he built by himself, off to hell and gone behind the new school."

"Keep an eye on Betty and on yourself."

"I will. Can't he get to you out there on the beach?"

"If he wants to try. And if I happen to stay there. But I won't. I'm going to buy some bug juice and some netting and scoop me a hole in the sand south of the cottage, down under the tree shadows. In case he comes calling."

"I'll stick close to Betty."

"Good deal."

chapter TEN

THE BIRDS woke Doyle in the first gray of dawn. He made a cautious inspection of the cottage and the surrounding area before going in with the blankets. By the time he had washed and shaved, the sun was beginning to cut the morning mist and promise a perfect day. The Gulf had quieted down.

Just as he was pouring a cup of coffee, he heard a racing engine approaching at high speed. He went to the back door. Buddy Larkin skidded to a stop in the pickup and scrambled out and ran heavily toward him, his strong face stamped with panic.

"Come on!" he said. "I'll tell you on the way. I think he's got Lucas and Betty too."

"How the hell did that happen?"

"Mom woke me up about an hour ago," Buddy said, backing the truck around recklessly. "She was worried because Betty hadn't come in."

"I thought you were going . . ."

"Hell, I did what you said. We all went to bed, about eleven I guess it was. He wouldn't come right into the house. Mom said when she woke me up that she heard voices down in the kitchen about two o'clock so she put on a robe and went down. Betty was down there, talking to Lucas Pennyweather. Mom said Lucas looked completely pooped. He said he'd done an awful lot of walking. Seems that Lucas was out in the side yard hollering to me. I sleep like I'm dead. Betty is a light sleeper. She heard him and got up."

They bounced almost clear of the road when they hit the crown of the wooden bridge.

"Lucas said he had come back and gone right to the Mack and run into Arnie Blassit, and Arnie said he was to get hold of me right away. So Lucas walked back to the house and he was calling me. Betty let him into the kitchen. Mom came down in time to hear Lucas telling her he was supposed to see me, but he didn't know what about. Betty told him it must be some kind of a mistake, that Arnie was probably drunk and got confused. By then it was a little after two. Lucas looked so tired Mom asked him to stay in the spare room. But he said no, he thought he'd be getting back to the Mack and get a ride on down with Arnie to the shack and get settled. He'd left his stuff on our back porch. Betty said he might miss Arnie.

"So nothing to do, but Betty decided she'd best drive the old man back to the Mack, and if Arnie had left, she'd drive him on down to Chaney's Bayou to the shack. Mom said Lucas looked pretty grateful. So Betty left in the jeep and I didn't hear a thing, damn it. Mom stayed awake. When Betty wasn't back quick, she figured she'd had to take the old man down to the shack. Finally she dozed off, and when she woke up again, about an hour ago, she looked out the window and the jeep wasn't there, and Betty wasn't in her bed, so she got nervous and woke me up."

They got out of the truck and hurried to the boat yard office. John Geer was sitting in the office looking unkempt and upset.

"Any luck?"

"He's flying a party over to Clewiston. They got word there for him to call here soon as he gets in. I couldn't get Daniels."

Buddy explained to Alex. "First thing I did was check and found his boat gone. His car is at Garner's. Got the glasses and got up onto the work-shed roof. Couldn't see a thing. Phoned the Coast Guard. But they're running a big air search for an outboard cruiser lost in the Gulf somewhere off Sarasota. I figure a plane search is the answer. Take a look at the chart."

A big chart was open on Betty's desk. Just south of the key bridge, the mainland cut sharply back, so that the bay became very wide. The marked channel hugged the bay shore of Ramona Key and Kelly Key. There was a bay area of ten miles long by an average of four miles wide to search, including the shore line of both keys and the mainland shore line. Forty square miles, so densely pocked with islands that a lot of it was like a great saltwater marsh, with winding tidal streams. He saw the oddly shaped indentation of Bucket Bay on the mainland side, eight miles down, opposite Kelly Key.

"Skippy Illman flies charter out of Fort Myers. He's got a good little twin-engine amphib. He's a friend, and once he phones in and gets the pitch, it won't take him long to get on down here. When will he phone in, John?"

"Fifteen or twenty minutes."

"I got hold of Lawlor and I told him just enough so he ought to come roaring over here with some of his people."

"Maybe he didn't take Betty with him."

"Then where the hell is she if he didn't? I found the jeep. In the lot behind the Mack. And then I came over to get you."

"Did you look around that area? Look thoroughly?"

Buddy swallowed with an obvious effort. "See what you mean. Let's go back. Stick by that phone, John."

They turned into the alley and parked beside the empty blue jeep. They looked into it. Buddy pointed at an old canvas duffle bag on the floor. "Didn't see that before. Belongs to Lucas, I guess."

Doyle heard a screen door bang and he turned and saw Janie, pasty and squinting in the morning sun, wearing a shiny green-satin housecoat with a ripped hem, come out with a bulging brown bag and stare at them curiously as she went over to a row of four lidless garbage cans buzzing with flies and dropped the bag in.

"What's going on?"

"Did you tend bar last night, Janie?" Buddy asked.

"Just till it got too rough and Harry made me quit. That was maybe nine."

"Is Harry around? I'd like to see him."

"I'll get him."

They quickly searched the brush around the perimeter of the parking lot. Harry came out in his underwear top, baggy cotton slacks, his belly hanging over his belt, the sun shining on the dark spots on his bald head, picking his teeth with a certain amount of daintiness.

"I looked out and seen your jeep earlier and wondered what the hell," Harry said.

"Did you see Lucas last night?"

Harry strolled over and stood by the jeep with them. "Hell, yes. The old basser made it all the way back. He talked to Arnie and then he took off after only one drink, and everybody in the place trying to buy him one."

"I suppose Donnie was in."

"Sure. He's always in and out a half dozen times on a Saturday night. Wisht he'd stay to hell away. He puts a gloom on the place. But he's sure handy when folks get troublesome."

"Harry, see if you can remember. I know how busy you are. How many times did Donnie come in after Lucas was here?"

"That ain't hard, because Lucas was here late. Half an hour before closing. Donnie come in one more time about quarter of, and everybody was still talking about old Lucas. I see him come in but I didn't see him go. He couldn't have stayed more than a minute. One of the times Donnie was in earlier, Gil Kemmer was in jawing at him and I was sure Donnie would take him out back and work him over but he didn't pay any attention to Gil. Seemed funny. Gil was sore on account of Donnie clubbing Lee Kemmer up so bad he had to be took off the road gang and put in the hospital over in Davis. The way I figure . . ."

"Thanks, Harry."

"Anything I can do, you just let me know." He walked back toward the screen door. He turned and said, "Say. Janie and me are going to get married, Buddy." Doyle saw the girl standing behind the screen and heard her giggle. It was a singularly empty sound.

And then, as he turned, something caught his eye. It was a brown smear on the sharp corner of the windshield frame. Adhering to it, and moving slightly in the east wind, was a small swath of hair, perhaps a dozen long glossy strands, ginger and cream, unmistakably hers.

Buddy examined it and then the men exchanged quick glances, as though involved in some kind of special shame, a climate of inner revulsion.

"Let's get back to the office," Buddy murmured.

John Geer shook his head dolefully as they walked in. Buddy said, "I'll take it. You go get that Prowler ready to roll. Take the aluminum dink off the Huckins next to it and just dump it in the cockpit. Put that little three-horse of mine on the dink and make sure it's gassed up."

John Geer loped off.

As soon as he was gone Buddy said, "This is just as rough on old John as it is on me. He'd follow her around like a dog if she'd let him."

The phone rang and he snatched it up. "Yeah? That's right. Hello! Skippy? We got trouble. I don't want to take time to explain. Need you for a search. All those bay islands to the south of us here. It's life and death, boy. Can you get over here fast? Good. I'll be out in the bay on a Prowler. White with blue trim. It's got a ship-to-who, and when you get close enough, you call me on the Coast Guard emergency channel and I'll tell you what to look for. You run that bird flat out, hear?"

He hung up. "It won't take him long."

John Geer had followed orders, and he had the twin engines of the fast little cabin cruiser turning over. They went aboard and Buddy took the controls while John Geer cast off the remaining lines. Doyle noticed that Geer had a pistol shoved into the waistband of his jeans. It looked like a twenty-two, possibly a Woodsman. Once they were clear of the docks, Buddy shoved the throttles forward. The boat came to life, the engines roaring in synchronization, the white bow cutting the blue morning water. They headed down the bay about four miles before Buddy throttled down. He sent John to the bow to throw over the small anchor. When it bit firm and the boat swung to rest in the tidal current at the edge of the channel, Buddy cut the motors, leaned below and turned on the ship-to-shore. From time to time, very faintly, they could pick up the routine reports of the search planes off Sarasota.

Doyle looked at the islands. They were unchanged from the days when the Caloosas had built their mounds there. Jungles of mangrove to the water's edge and, where they were high enough, clumps of cabbage palm, some live oaks on the bigger ones.

Sunday fishing traffic passed them, and people waved casually.

"If you fixed the motor," Doyle asked, "could he get to where he was going?"

"Running at night it would be cooler. It wouldn't heat up so fast. He might make four miles. He might make ten. Depends on how fast. And at night he'd run slower. He could get where he's going, maybe. He might have gone into the islands and then waited for daylight so old Lucas could guide him the rest of the way. It would have time maybe to cool down so it would start again. But even if it didn't, he had a paddle in there. If he took Betty along, I guess he figured on running. But he won't get out of there fast with that motor. I wish to God I hadn't buggered up the motor now. Maybe he would have just left them there. But if he's stuck . . ."

"Shut up, please, Buddy," John Geer said and turned away.

"*Slow Goose* calling Larkin on the Prowler," a drawling voice came in, startlingly loud and clear. Buddy jumped for the hand mike.

"Larkin on the *Aces Up,* come in, Skippy."

"*Slow Goose* to the *Aces Up,* I'm halfway from Davis, boy, and you should spot me soon. Where are you? Over."

"*Aces Up* to the *Slow Goose,* I'm about a mile northeast of Windy Pass anchored beside the channel. Look for a twelve-foot aluminum boat with a bright red motor on it. Check the islands and the shore lines. If it's pulled up under the trees we may be out of luck, but you might still be able to spot that motor. There can be one person in it or two or three. One is a woman. Betty, if you want to know. And in one hell of a jam, boy. Over."

"Coast Guard to the *Aces Up* and the *Slow Goose.* This is an emergency channel reserved for Coast Guard use. Vacate the emergency channel."

"*Aces Up* to the Coast Guard operator. This is an emergency. Repeat. This is an emergency. We're using a private search plane because you people are busy on something else. This is the only channel we have in common with the search plane. Will continue to use emergency channel, but we'll keep it as short as we can. Over."

"Coast Guard operator to the *Aces Up.* No authority here to grant permission. But no way to stop you. Good luck. Over."

"There he is!" John Geer called. Doyle saw the small amphib coming at them at low altitude, coming from a point just south of Ramona.

The small aircraft gleamed in the morning sun. He buzzed the boat and climbed high.

"Slow Goose to the *Aces Up.* I'll take it high first and if no dice, I'll make a low square search. I'll give you the word. Over."

They stood at the rail and watched the high slow pattern, squinting up against the brightness of the sky. Time passed with a sickening slowness.

"What the hell is he doing?" Buddy snarled. No one answered.

Suddenly the plane tilted and dropped, leaf-lazy in the sun. It swung up again and began a wide slow circle.

"Slow Goose to *Aces Up,"* the voice drawled. "Got your customer, Buddy boy. He's in the middle of a little round bay right under me. Trying to start the motor apparently. He's stopped now. Paddling toward shore. Fella in khaki with a kind of a cowboy hat on him. What now? Over."

"We've got to get to him, Skippy. Fast as we can. Can you tell us how to get in there? Over."

"Slow Goose to *Aces Up.* Damn if I can tell you how, boy. I noticed you got a dinghy. If you run south to the channel marker south of the pass and leave the big boat there, you'll be close as you can get with it. Then you head in between those two bigger islands and turn right and . . . Damn, boy, it's a mess down there. Tell you what. Once you get going in the dinghy, I'll be Lura, the girl guide. When you got a turn to make, I'll tilt a wing at it, flying right at you or away from you as the case may be. Only way I can see to get you through that mess. And some places you may have to wade. I see deeper water here and there, but I don't know how the cowboy got in there. Over."

"Just get us in there, Skippy. Over and out."

They ran up to the marker. John waited for Buddy to edge the boat into the shallows beyond the channel and then dropped anchor. They dropped the dinghy over

the transom and climbed down into it. Three big men
badly overcrowded the eight-foot dinghy. John Geer ran
the small motor. It started on the first pull, and, at
its meager top speed, it made a sound like a small and
diligent hornet. Buddy knelt forward. Doyle had the middle seat.

As soon as they went between the two islands Skippy
had indicated, they were in flats so shallow that Geer
had to tilt the motor until the blade was thrashing half
out of water for a few moments until it deepened again.
The plane shadow swept over them and they followed
the tilt of the wing. The guiding system worked. Doyle
quickly lost track of the turns. They were in the narrow
tidal channels that cut the low land into islands. Needle
fish darted away in alarm. Blue herons stared with a
fierce amber eye, then flapped slowly away. Doyle saw a
water snake swimming near shore. Several times they had
to step out and pull the dinghy across shallows and
then start it again. As they walked in the shallows they
shuffled their feet to minimize the chance of getting hit
by a sting ray.

At last they came into an irregular open bay. Skippy
flew directly over a dense shore line of mangrove and
dipped the port wing. They couldn't believe there was an
opening there. They were almost on it before they saw it.
The water was deep and sleek and green. The channel
was narrow. At places the leaves touched overhead and
they were in mottled shadow, ducking under limbs.

Doyle thought of the child who had been brought here
long ago, sitting in her pink dress in the bow of the skiff,
full of a child's love for secrets and sense of adventure.
If this was the right place.

The channel writhed and abruptly opened onto an almost circular bay a hundred yards across. Geer throttled
down abruptly. The aircraft had climbed high again.

"There's the boat," Buddy said softly, an unnecessary
comment. They had all seen it, the gleam of aluminum

and the red motor in the shade where it had been drawn up, empty, directly across the bay from the single entrance. With the small motor barely turning over, the dinghy moved very slowly.

"Old shack over there," John Geer murmured. "See it under the trees. Little to the right of the boat."

"I see it," Buddy said. "Cleared off a long time ago but it's grown up. Good high ground. Cabbage palm."

Doyle felt dangerously exposed. Above the muted burbling of the small outboard he heard the sliding click as Geer worked a shell into the chamber of the target pistol.

"Where the hell is he?" Geer whispered. "I don't like this."

"Move it up a little closer," Buddy ordered.

They could see the small shack more distinctly. The warped door had fallen out of the frame and there was a sagging shutter on the single window.

"She used to tell how he'd take her to a stone castle full of jewels and she was a princess," Buddy said.

"Look to the left of the boat," Doyle said. "About fifteen feet from it." The figure was in shadows. It was face down over the mangrove roots, and utterly still. There were sun dollars on the faded back of the blue work shirt. The back of the white head was out of water.

Geer whispered, "If he killed old Lucas like that, we better figure on coming in here with more than just one little . . ."

The three shots were authoritative, heavy-throated, evenly spaced. They had a flat sound in the stillness, and were harsh in that special way that can happen only when you are in line with the muzzle. Merged with the middle shot, Doyle heard the once-heard-never-forgotten sound of a slug smashing into flesh and bone. He plunged over the side of the dinghy into two feet of shallow water, turned and grasped the dinghy as the slow-turning motor threatened to move it away. Buddy had plunged out of the dinghy too, but stayed on his feet. And, with ponderous strength, ran diagonally toward the shore, angling away from the cabin, head down and knees high. There was a shiny red-black stain on the back of Buddy's right shoulder, spreading as he ran. There was another shot but Buddy kept running. He dived headlong into the mangroves about sixty feet from the shack, and about a hundred feet from the dinghy.

Doyle had turned the dinghy so that it was between him and the shack. He pushed it until he was near the stern, and then pulled down on the near gunwale so as to tip the far side up to give him cover as he reached and turned the motor off. With the dinghy tilted he could see John Geer crumpled in the bottom of it. He could see his face. The slug had entered just above the left eyebrow, hammering a black, round, lethal hole delicately rimmed with a froth of blood.

The aircraft sound grew loud, and the amphib came down so low that Doyle thought for a moment the man was going to attempt a landing in the tiny bay. But it lifted and cleared the trees at the end, and droned away until the sound of it was lost. The bay was still. He heard a sleepy sound of birds, a heat-whine of insects, a crashing in the thick brush where Buddy had disappeared.

"John?" Buddy's call was loud in the stillness.

"He's dead," Doyle called back.

After a long silence Buddy called, with pain and hoarse anger in his voice, "What are you trying to do, Donnie? You crazy bastard! You can't kill everybody in the world! Where's Betty?"

There was no answer. "Are you hurt, Alex?"

"No."

"I think I got it bad. I think he smashed hell out of my right shoulder. I'm beginning to feel kind of funny. There's a lot of blood. Where do you think he is?"

"Near the shack. But I'm not sure."

"Maybe he's working his way toward me. I've hunted with him. He can move without a sound. Where's John?"

"In the dinghy."

"Where's his gun?"

"Maybe it's under him. I'll see if I can find it."

"Don't get careless. Don't give him a chance at you."

It was difficult to shift the body. He saw the muzzle under Geer's left thigh. He tilted the dinghy further and worked the gun out. He opened his mouth to call to Buddy that he had it, and then changed his mind. He waited a few minutes longer. Then he called, "Buddy."

"Yes?" The reply was alarmingly weak.

"I can't find it. I guess he dropped it over the side when he was hit."

"Then you . . . better . . . try to get out of here. I . . . can't. . . . Things are fading."

He checked the gun. The safety was off.

"Doyle!" It was Capp's voice, coming from the vicinity of the shack.

"What do you want, Mister Deputy, sir?"

"I want that little boat, Doyle. You shove it into shore nice, and I'll leave you healthy. I have to come get it and you'll be dead as the rest of 'em."

The final phrase made Doyle's heart sink. Up until that moment there had been frail hope. Now there was no room within him for anything but an anger so great that for a moment it blurred his vision.

"You haven't got a damn thing to lose by letting me have it too, Donnie. What guarantee have I got?"

"You took too much time, Doyle. You lost a chance. I'm coming after it."

He knew what the dinghy meant to Capp. With it he could get to the mainland. With his knowledge of the sloughs and swamps, he had a chance to get away. He heard a slow sloshing sound and knew that Donnie was wading out toward him. He could visualize him, the pale watchful eyes, the revolver ready. And he wouldn't want to take a chance on holing the dinghy.

Doyle weighed his chances. They were not good. He knew that he could put at least one hole in Capp, but one little twenty-two slug was not going to prevent Capp firing at least once, and from a range that would make a miss unlikely. And the impact of that slug would make the chance of a second hole in Donnie Capp very unlikely.

His only possible chance, he knew, would be to make Capp lose some of his animal caution. And so, as rapidly as he could without exposing himself in any way, Doyle began to scuttle backward in the deepening water, pulling the dinghy with one hand, holding the target pistol in his right.

Capp gave a grunt of surprise and anger, and, as Doyle continued to pull, he heard the thrashing, splashing sound of Capp running through the shallow water to overtake the boat before Doyle could reach the entrance to the bay.

It was difficult to guess by the sounds when Capp would be at the optimum distance. There would be no time to aim. And if he made his move at a moment when Capp's gun hand was swung forward in the effort of running through the water, one snap shot could end it.

When it seemed that Capp was almost near enough to touch the boat, Doyle got his feet under him, thrust the dinghy violently to one side and came to his feet in water almost to his waist, and saw Capp fifteen feet away plunging toward him. He had no conscious awareness of aiming. He did not hear the snapping of the shots. He merely kept the muzzle centered on Capp's chest and kept pulling the trigger. Donnie Capp blundered to a stop with a look of wild and vacant surprise on his seamed and sallow face. It was that inimitable look, the look a man uses but once in a lifetime. The look of the ultimate surprise.

Still off balance Capp thrust the heavy revolver forward and fired once. He got his balance and lowered the revolver slowly and fired again, down into the water beside his leg. As Doyle fired, he saw the small black spots appearing by magic in the faded khaki shirt. The gaudy deputy shield clinked and whined away.

Capp sat down in the water slowly, as though with deliberate caution. He stared at Doyle and then, suddenly, the look of surprise faded. And he was staring beyond the unknown stars. He toppled over onto his side, straightened out, made a slow half roll onto his face and sank, very slowly, to the bottom. The pale hat floated, right side up.

Doyle looked down at the gun in his hand. He lowered it. He trudged woodenly to the dinghy, dropped the gun in beside John Geer's body, and towed the dinghy ashore and beached it beside Capp's boat. And then he walked along the shore line in the water to the place where Buddy had dived into cover.

Buddy lay on his back, his face wet and gray, his lips blue. Doyle ripped the bloody shirt from the wound. It was blood from shoulder to waist. He took off his own shirt and, ripping long strips and fashioning two pads, he tightly bound the small entrance wound and the great torn hole in the rear. He made the binding tighter by using John Geer's belt. He felt the huge man's pulse. It felt frail and uncertain. There was nothing more he could do for him. He did not dare move him.

He went back to where the boats were. He took Lucas's ankles and dragged him back out of the water. He had seen the crabs hurry away when he pulled the old man out, so he left him face down in the heavy grass.

He turned then, slowly, and took a deep breath and let it out and walked up toward the shack, looking to left and right for the body of the girl.

She lay face down in heavy undergrowth to the left of the shack. He saw the white of her skirt and went over to her. The skirt was rumpled and dirty, and hiked above the brown knees. One foot was bare, a sandal on the other one. She lay, toeing in, one arm under her body. There was a large area behind and above her right ear where the heavy-textured hair was matted with dark dried blood. A red ant crawled across the small of her brown back, where the yellow blouse had hiked up out of the waist of the skirt.

He looked bitterly down at her and knew it was only the greatness of his need that made him think he saw a faint movement, as though she breathed. Suddenly and breathlessly, he dropped to his knees and laid his ear against the back of the yellow blouse. And heard then the slow and vital cadence of her heart, the deep and healthy thudding of the life in her. When he straightened up he was smiling like a fool, and the tears were running down his face.

He rolled her tenderly and carefully onto her back, and smoothed out her skirt and brushed her hair back from her forehead. He tore the pocket out of his trousers and rinsed it in salt water and used that to gently cleanse the grime and bits of twigs from her face. He kissed her unconscious lips.

After what seemed a very long time he heard the aircraft again, moving back and forth, pointing out the channels to someone else. Finally it was close. He could look up and catch glimpses of it through the leaves. It went away then and he heard the sound of motors and the voices of many men. He walked down and watched them come across the bay toward him.

chapter ELEVEN

DOYLE, on the first day of May, walked out of the Davis General Hospital with Betty Larkin. He had driven her over to see Buddy. Buddy had been in a wheel chair on the sun porch, his smashed shoulder in a curious and complicated cast. And he had been restless and in a vile mood, convinced that everything at the yard was going to hell.

They walked across to the parking lot. Betty wore a beige dress with aqua buttons on the pockets. She wore a scarf over her head to hide the place where her hair had been shaved away so that the wound made by Donnie's club could be stitched.

She was subdued, thoughtful.

After he had turned onto the road to Ramona, she said, "So you're all packed."

"Just about. Not much to pack."

"And you've got your reservation."

"Tomorrow at ten out of Tampa. I'll have to get a darn early start to unload this heap before I have to be at the airport."

"I could drive up with you, Alex. You could make the title over to me and I could sell it and send you the money."

"I wouldn't want to ask you to go to all that trouble."

"After what you did for us? Good Lord, Alex! And you won't even let us give you a dime of the money."

"What's the word on that, anyway?"

"Oh, you know those fruit jars where the rubber had rotted and water had got in, and the money was just a mass of glop? The lawyer says it will go to Washington

155

where experts work on it, and he thinks we may get an almost hundred per cent recovery. We have no idea how much there is in those jars. And he says that the tax people are prepared to be reasonable. We may be able to keep quite a lot."

"I hope so."

"It would be nice to be out of hock on all the improvements we made. Poor John Geer. He said so many times that when we finally paid off the bank, he was going to get drunk."

"Are you still sore at me for lying to you in the beginning about why I came down?"

"No. I was sort of irritated. But I understand. If you remember, my friend, there were flaws in your performance. And I noticed them, too."

"So you did. Smart gal."

"It's nice to see you relaxed, Alex. You were so strained and nervous-acting."

"Because I was back here, mostly. I didn't want to come back. I felt this place had a hex on me."

"Boy leaves in disgrace. Man comes back and becomes big hero. Gets in all the papers. Becomes public figure."

"All right. I enjoy it, damn it. I enjoy walking down Bay Street and getting the big glad hand from end to end of it."

"You won't take any of the money?"

"How many times are you going to ask? No! Thanks."

She turned sideways in the seat. "I want to tell you something. When I went to the bank and looked at all that money there on that table, something happened to me. Maybe I lost a hex. I'd thought of Daddy as something larger than life. I never saw him in perspective, the way you are supposed to see your parents after you grow up. He kept on being a big, cold, watchful eye looking down at me from up in the clouds somewhere. Making me feel clumsy and guilty and ashamed. And then I saw the money. And I thought of him sneaking away in the skiff and squirreling that money away in fruit jars in the ground, scared to death somebody would follow him or catch him at it. Something sort of went click. He wasn't big and cold and frightening any more. He was just a scared, greedy, twisted little man. The only thing that really mattered in that shriveled little soul was the money. Not Jenna. She was a pretty toy. And the hex faded. I feel sorry for him. I'm trying to understand him, Alex. He had so very little to start with. And it hurt him. But why should it hurt him? You had almost as little. You've done well. And you aren't all . . . withered up inside the way he was."

"Maybe I am, in some other way."

"Nonsense!"

"I mean it. I avoid emotions. I avoid emotional responsibilities, Betty. They scare me. That's part of why I had to be forced, or I would never have come back."

She did not answer.

"Drop you at home?" he asked.

"Please. And if you don't mind, I'll jeep over later for a swim and get the spare key back, and see you haven't left anything around, such as a toothbrush."

She came out and swam, and she seemed particularly gay, joyous in a rather high-keyed way. After they had changed and were having a sunset drink on the porch, she went out to the jeep and came back with a package for him. He opened it, with protests.

"It's from Mom and Buddy and me, but I picked it out. It's the dangdest one I ever saw. It tells time, I think, if you can find the right hands to look at. But see all these little levers and things? With this you can do anything. But you better read the instructions."

"It's very handsome, and I thank you. Please thank your mother and Buddy for me." He put it on.

"What will you do with this old one?"

"Throw it away, I guess."

She put it in the pocket of her skirt. "I think I'll keep it. I'm a sentimental type. I'll put it with that old diary where you're featured so strongly. Mind?"

"If you want it. I don't know why you should want it. All it does is tell time, and it doesn't do that very well."

"Which I had noticed and which I remembered." She put her glass on the railing. "Want me to drive up with you tomorrow?"

"I'll manage, thanks."

"So walk me out to the jeep and say good-by, Alex."

They walked around the cottage to the blue jeep waiting in patience in the heavy dusk.

"You will come back, won't you? Sometime?"

He looked at her standing there. And the need to say things was strong inside him, trying to break free. I will come back, to see you. Because I don't think I can go very long from here on without seeing you once in a while.

But he heard himself say, too casually, "I suppose I'll be back to look at the town. I don't know when, Betty."

"Oh, Alex!" she said in a choked voice, and he looked quickly at her and saw that there was just enough light to make the tear tracks on her cheeks gleam. She held her arms out toward him shyly, tentatively.

He took her in his arms strongly, with a sound in his throat like a sob, and then he could say the words. Something how he felt when he thought her dead. How he would come back often, and only to be with her for a little while.

And then he kissed her. He felt again the resistance, her fright, the dead stiffness of mouth. And just as he was about to release her in despair, her taut body began to relax, and there was a stir and a change in the texture of h. She reached to put her arm awkwardly around She kissed him back meagerly, and then more d then suddenly with a great strong overwhelm- She pushed away from him and stared at him with her eyes wide and streaming, her lips tremulous.

"Pow!" she said softly, ludicrously. And came back strenuously for more. And backed away again, taking a quick step to regain her balance and said, "I feel dizzy. And I don't feel the least dang bit scared. Or crawly. Or anything like that. I feel like I'd all of a sudden turned into a big pile of warm raspberry Jello."

"I love you."

"Don't be silly! What else could feel like this? I love you too. More, please."

With the next kiss, her warm brown arms were strong, and she made a guttural purring sound deep in her throat, and she bruised her mouth and his. And so she went home and she came back, and they walked and talked, with pauses for kisses, until dawn. There was lots of time coming for more than kisses, and this was the time to catch up on all of those that she had missed. She drove to Tampa with him, because he had to go back, at least this time. And by then it had been agreed that because she was a marriageable girl with perhaps plenty of money, he'd be very smart to marry her. He would go up and check on the next assignment and wangle something where a wife could be taken along, and also get enough time off to come down and marry her and take her back with him. And in the meantime she would have a chance to find a very bright girl for the office so Buddy wouldn't miss her too much. Then after she had her taste of far places, and probably enough kids to make traveling a major problem, he would have his twenty years in and they would come back to Ramona and buy on the beach and build there and drive Buddy nuts helping him run the Larkin-Doyle Boat Yard and Marina.

It seemed remarkably easy to organize the rest of your life. No trick at all.

He waved from the top of the ramp as he got onto the plane.

At first when the stewardess walked down the aisle t

ward him, she smiled broadly. By the time they were over Georgia he thought she was looking at him rather strangely.

And it was then that he discovered that he was still wearing a big, broad, idiotic smile, fringed with lipstick.